MW00827550

SIEGE OF
THE HEART

Sheryl McDanel Munson

A KISMET ™ Romance

METEOR

TM

METEOR PUBLISHING CORPORATION
Bensalem, Pennsylvania

To Vicky and Star,
for their tireless support, assistance and encouragement and to Gwen, for her blind faith.

SHERYL McDANEL MUNSON

After the "New Austerity" rendered my M.A. in Art History virtually unmarketable, I worked in a number of unrelated fields for seven years before I began teaching art at a local college. My husband and I are remodeling a house that we hope will be within the confines of a proposed national park in eastern Pennsylvania, finding new homes for sour dough starter, and trying to breed the most uncooperative pair of finches in existence.

ONE

It was all Julie's fault, Courtney Welsch reminded herself as she rubbed the aching spot at the base of her spine. It was always Julie's fault. After a ten year friendship with Julie, she should have recognized the idea as the crock it was the second she heard it. But had she? Of course not; she never did. Once Julie got going, flying to the moon started to make sense. Sound reasonable. Even desirable. And every time she tried to fly and failed, Julie just stood there with that infuriatingly innocent expression on her face that dared Courtney to blame her. The fact that Taylor was just as susceptible to Julie's suggestions as she was wasn't a consolation this time; she was the one that had to live with the consequences of this particular brainstorm.

She didn't even like skiing, for pity's sake. She didn't like snow or cold either, for that matter. As far as she was concerned, winter's only redeeming aspects were sweaters.

Julie, however, loved to ski.

Neither her husband nor her best friend had ever begrudged her that interest; they both just wished she had the decency to leave them out of it. And Courtney never wished it more fervently than she did at the moment. If she had never let Julie talk her into that cursed trip, she never would have gone skiing, never would have broken her foot, and never would have met Nick Trielo.

It had been the second day of their one-week trip to the Poconos; January and cold and wet and thoroughly disgusting. After five terror-filled minutes—if that—on the bunny slope, Courtney had caught her ski tip on some invisible monster lurking beneath the snow, fallen, and twisted her foot. She had known something was broken even before Julie and Taylor took her to the hospital. Afterward, Taylor, empathetic because it could just as easily have been him, bought her every Stephen King novel he could lay his hands on, and installed her and her cast in the gigantic conversation pit in the lodge's lounge with a Walkman, her David Bowie tapes, and a thermos full of hot buttered rum.

It did help. Sort of. But none of Taylor's well-intentioned offerings made her forget that Julie was ultimately responsible for her dilemma.

Precisely at that nadir of her existence, that hunk Nick Trielo and his cast hobbled into the cavernous lounge and her life. From the moment he first prodded her shoulder with the rubber tip of his crutches, she'd been lost.

Lord, what a mountain. If they'd cover him with snow, *then* she might consider skiing a worthwhile pursuit. The mere thought of sliding over that spectacular body sent an involuntary shiver through her.

Nick possessed the chest and shoulders of the Colossus of Rhodes and thighs like redwood trunks. Not that she'd ever actually seen a redwood before it became a picnic table, but she just knew that they started out resembling Nick's legs. Huge as he was, there wasn't an excess inch or ounce on him. He was undeniably solid, incredibly fit, and definitively masculine.

"Hi." It wasn't much as far as memorable greetings went, but in her speechless state, she felt grateful that she could summon that much.

"Hi."

She blinked in astonishment at the sound of the single word. It sounded as if it came all the way from his toes.

"Could I join you?"

Could he? He could not only join her, he could commit twelve indecent acts before she recovered her senses. If she recovered her senses. And she wasn't sure she wanted to.

"Yes."

With effortless ease that belied the fifty-or-so pounds of plaster on his leg, Nick lowered himself to the edge of the pit and slid down beside her. His body was even more fantastic in motion than it was standing still. The hard shoulder that brushed lightly against hers barely touched it, but she felt as if the fleeting contact had knocked every cubic inch of air from her lungs. Raggedly, she struggled to draw another breath through her mouth. If she didn't get control of herself soon, she was going to be the one committing indecent acts.

Ignoring Nick's devastating looks turned out to be easier than she had anticipated. Apparently, she wasn't his type. Courtney speculated that a man like Nick could be minutely specific about his type and get precisely what he ordered. At first, it had been more than a little disappointing. To be honest, her self-esteem had taken a hard shot to the jaw. After all, it wasn't as if she were a troll. There just wasn't anything terribly remarkable about her. And once they got past the fact that Nick was remarkable and she wasn't, they got along just fine. As friends. And only friends.

It was really ironic. There she was, at one of the most exciting, romantic resorts in the Poconos, with one of the most gorgeous men she had seen in her life. While every other woman in the place was skiing, ice skating, tobogganing, and swimming in the indoor pool, all the while pursuing Mr. Right, Courtney sat with Nick in the conversation pit and talked, played cards and backgammon, and drank hot buttered rum. For this, she could have stayed at home and invited her next-door neighbors in for the evening.

Nick lay on the bed in a hotel room in Chicago and wondered, not for the first time in the last fourteen weeks, what he was going to do about Courtney. They hadn't parted on the best of terms, to say the least, and he guessed he couldn't blame her. He had probably deserved every last one of the colorful names she'd called him just before she'd clobbered him with the Orrefors and shoved him out the door of her apartment.

He decided that he must have masochistic tendencies he'd never suspected before. There wasn't any other explanation for it. The woman had told him to get lost in no uncertain terms—she'd hit him with a good solid hunk of lead crystal, for God's sake—and he didn't have enough sense to listen to her. But then everything about his relationship with Court had been out of character right from the start.

With a dogged persistence that had surprised even him, he'd tried to call her, tried to explain, but she'd changed her telephone number and the new one was unlisted. Since then, he'd sent cards every day and flowers from every single city he'd been in. Court had ignored them all.

He'd even tried talking to Julie and Taylor, but Julie had called him a few names that Court had missed and Taylor said that he intended to stay as far away from this mess as was humanly possible. He couldn't really blame them. They were Court's best friends, and they were being admirably loyal to her. He just wished that one of them would break down and assure him that she still lived in the same place because when he got back to New York the week after next, he intended to give it yet another try.

What he really wished, more than anything, was that he had told her the truth when they first met, before he realized that he was in love with her, when they were still friends, not lovers. At the time, though, it hadn't seemed important. Foolish him.

The trip to the Poconos had been his first real vacation in two years and he'd taken it in spite of heated objections from his manager, Jake. Jake had been even angrier with him when he'd heard about the accident. Actually, he'd been furious with Nick and he'd all but accused him of breaking his leg on purpose, just to extend his vacation. It never occurred to Jake that no one in his right mind would do a thing like that, particularly on what was only the third day of a long-awaited ski vacation.

He had just gotten off the phone after yet another screaming argument with Jake and decided to get out of the room before Jake called him back to yell some more. The lounge, he told himself. If Jake had him paged, he wouldn't have to answer it.

Three days on the crutches was accomplishing something. He was getting around much better. If he didn't get a bath soon, though, he was going to lose his mind. Not to mention friends. He tried to ignore how gamy he was starting to feel. No one else would be able to.

It wasn't as if he were going to be meeting anyone in the lounge, after all, he consoled himself. Not in the morning, anyway. Everyone else was out on the slopes. He might as well have stayed in his room alone, except he wanted to avoid Jake and he was starting to get cabin fever. And the pit was more comfortable than anything in his room, even if the most exciting things on the agenda were a book he'd already read and hot buttered rum.

If he hadn't been so preoccupied with Jake, his boredom, and the intricacies of dealing with crutches and a hefty chunk of plaster, he would have noticed sooner that he wasn't alone in the lounge. He was slipping, definitely slipping. He couldn't remember walking into a room and not noticing a woman being there since puberty.

He made his way as close to the side of the conversation

pit as he dared, craned his neck, and peered down at her curiously.

Damn, Nick thought idly. She wasn't his type. Not his type at all.

The riot of shiny black curls poking above the rim of the pit had given him hopes, but they were dashed at once. Her skin wasn't just creamy, it was pale. No one who went skiing had skin that white. No one who was still alive had skin that white. The rest of her was, at best, uninspiring. She was wearing a corduroy OshKosh bib jumper over an Icelandic wool sweater over a turtleneck. If there were a body underneath all the bulk, it would take a week to find it.

Okay, okay, so she wasn't the woman of his dreams. He couldn't help it if he had a weakness for golden blondes. Not skinny little white-faced porcelain dolls who hid beneath twenty pounds of wool. No one said he had to keep her. At least she was someone to talk to. If she'd been sitting there long, she'd probably be grateful for some company. Maybe even some hot buttered rum.

Shifting his weight onto his good left leg, Nick reached one crutch out to nudge her shoulder lightly. Her head tipped back in response and she looked up at him.

It was a revelation. Lord, what eyes. They couldn't really be that color, but they were. Violet. Deep, dark violet, like everyone said that Elizabeth Taylor's were, but he'd never believed it. Rimmed by the thickest, darkest, curliest lashes he had ever seen, they were huge in her pale face. He had a sudden inexplicable urge to wallow in them.

The bizzare notion passed when he remembered that she wasn't his type.

"Courtney, are you all right? You look a little pale. Maybe you should go home. At least lie down for a while. I'll run interference for you."

"Maggie, you worry too much. I'm fine." As if to

prove that she was telling the truth, Courtney forced herself to smile at her secretary.

"Don't you give me that 'fine' garbage, young lady, because it won't wash with me. You aren't eating right, are you?"

"Do you want to hear the menu for last night's dinner? Tonight's?"

"I want you to take care of yourself." Maggie Kline frowned at her boss again. Maybe Courtney Welsch was an influential investments analyst, but there were times when she really needed a keeper. "I'll get you a glass of milk."

"I don't want a glass of milk."

"You'll drink it anyway. I'll get it." The matter was settled.

Courtney scowled at Maggie's receding back. Sometimes the woman thought she was her mother instead of her secretary. She certainly acted like it, anyway.

Which was why she had to answer her own telephone, she muttered to herself as the offending instrument rang. "Welsch speaking."

"Court, it's me."

Julie. Just what she needed at the moment, Courtney told herself sarcastically. What was she going to talk her into now, sky diving? Lion taming?

"Were your ears burning?"

"Were you talking about me?"

"No, but I was certainly thinking enough to make your ears burn."

"How are you feeling?"

"Is that the $64,000 question for the day?" If one more person asked her how she was feeling, Courtney was going to scream.

"Speaking of cranky, Nick called. He sounded as ill-tempered as you do."

"Did you tell him to go throw someone over the ropes and he'd feel better?"

"Court, you ought to talk to him."

"What good would that do?" She answered her own question. "None, absolutely none."

"You used to like to talk to Nick."

"That was when he was still my friend."

Their conversation had been so easy then. Almost from the first, they'd been able to talk to one another as if they'd been friends for years. They'd understood each other's jokes. Even the ones that weren't funny. Even the ones that didn't make sense.

"What did you do to break your leg?"

He laughed. It was light, self-deprecating. "Tried to ski on ice. You?"

"Tried to ski, period."

"Ski often?"

"As little as possible. I hate cold, snow, and sports. Not necessarily in that order. I wanted to go to Jamaica. Cancun. Tahiti. I wasn't being picky. Really. Any place with sun and sand would have been fine with me. The Sahara would have been perfect."

"Why didn't you go there, then?"

"Julie. My alleged best friend."

"Julie likes to ski." Nick completed the thought for her.

"Taylor and I tried to convince her that our feelings wouldn't be hurt if she left us at home and came by herself. She wouldn't listen to us."

They'd known each other for less than fifteen minutes when they had that conversation, but they could complete each other's thoughts and sentences already, as if they were able to read one another's minds.

Courtney had hoped that Nick couldn't read everything that was in her mind. He was absolutely gorgeous, there were no two ways about it. A woman would have to be dead not to respond to that. A lesser woman would have jumped his bones in the first three minutes. Courtney, recognizing his lack of interest, had repressed that urge;

she merely gawked at him surreptitiously for the next three days while they had played at being friends.

"He wants to marry you."

"That's what all the cards say."

"Are you still getting them?"

"Every day."

"Are you saving them?"

Courtney didn't answer; her silence said volumes.

"Are the flowers still coming, too?"

"Yes."

"How can you resist anything that romantic?"

"He lied to me."

"Call him." The telephone number where he could be reached was always on the cards.

"No. And don't you tell him."

"Even I wouldn't go that far. It isn't fair of you not to tell him, you know."

"What does fair have to do with anything where Nick Trielo is concerned? He lied to me, Julie."

Courtney remembered exactly when the lie had started. They had been exchanging all the pertinent information that people do when they first meet one another. They had just discovered their mutual addiction to Stephen King, and she had lamented the fact that her job occupied so much of her time that it was difficult for her to get a chance to read.

"What do you do?"

"I'm an investments analyst."

"Stocks and bonds and IRAs and mutual funds and that sort of thing?"

She nodded. "It's interesting."

He smiled, shrugged, and shook his head. "I don't understand any of it. You tell people how to make money with the money they've already got."

"You do understand it."

"You have just heard the full extent of my knowledge on the subject."

"What do you do?"

"I'm an investment." And then he'd given her that big adorable grin and she'd forgotten all about it.

"Court? Court? Are you still there?" Julie's voice carried through the receiver demandingly.

"Yes, Julie." Courtney sighed. "My mind was just wandering."

"I certainly hope it was wandering to that gorgeous hunk. You know, if I thought he'd have me, I'd drop Taylor in a minute."

"Want him? He's yours."

"I was kidding, and you know it, Court. Not that he isn't a hunk, mind you. He doesn't want me, anyway. He wants you back."

"Drop it, Julie. Please?"

"You're my best friend, Court, but you're being an idiot."

"Nick? Nick? Nicky!" the voice demanded, yanking him back into the present and reality.

"Hmm?" His head shot up. "Oh. You were saying something, Steve?"

"Nick, if you don't stop daydreaming, one of us is going to get hurt. And I'm really afraid it's going to be me."

"Sorry."

Steve rolled his eyes heavenward, pleading for divine assistance. "I suppose this is how you broke your leg."

"No. It happened before."

"So call her."

"She changed her number. It's unlisted now. Besides, she won't talk to me."

"So forget her."

"I can't."

"She wasn't your type, anyway."

"I know." Leaning against the rope, Nick rubbed his palm over the tattoo as if he were trying to erase it.

He recalled the first time Court had seen it. In the course of their peculiar conversation, he had learned that she was in precisely the same fix as he was. With the cast on his right leg, he needed a right-handed tub to dangle his leg over the side and keep his cast dry; with Court's cast on her left leg, she needed a left-handed tub. The tub in his room was left-handed; the one in her room was right-handed. It was mutually advantageous for them to use one another's bathtubs.

He emerged from her bathroom clad only in a pair of sweat pants, feeling infinitely better after his first bath in four days. It reaffirmed his faith that he was human. With his hip propped against the dresser, his crutches leaning against its end, he reached for the clean sweatshirt that lay there.

"Nick, what in God's name is that?"

Still supported by the dresser, he turned and looked over at Courtney, who was seated in a chair near the window. She was staring, her violet eyes filled with fascinated horror, at the tattoo on his chest, situated midway between his collarbone and his left nipple.

"What's it look like?"

"It looks like a tattoo."

"It is a tattoo."

"Oh." She was staring as it as if it were a snake. It wasn't; it was a skull and crossbones, and it wasn't very big. "Why?"

He grinned sheepishly. "I was nineteen, drunk, and with three of my fraternity brothers when we got them."

"But why a skull and crossbones?"

"It's the center of our fraternity crest." He shrugged lazily. "It seemed like a good idea at the time. Didn't you ever do anything strange when you were in school?"

"Never anything that strange."

He should have known then. If she couldn't understand something foolish that he'd done when he was just a kid, she'd never understand what he did for a living now.

"Nick, are you in there?" Steve's voice demanded, intruding into his thoughts.

Nick shook his head to clear it. "Sorry."

"Look, pal, if you're going to float off like this, I don't want you there on Saturday. One of us is going to get hurt. Get out of here. I'll find someone to fill in for you."

"I'll be fine."

"You will not be fine. Go back to New York tonight. Settle this thing once and for all. I'll see you when I get there week after next."

Courtney was not having the greatest of days. Actually, on a scale of one to ten, it had been a negative twenty. She felt so lousy when she awakened that she'd briefly considered calling in sick; she couldn't do that, though, not when they were considering her for the junior partnership, in spite of everything. She had to prove to McGuinn, McGuinn, McGuinn, and Becker that she could do it all—and do it all well.

With grim determination, she'd dragged herself out of bed only to discover that nothing she owned was ironed. Her feet, swollen with the first disgustingly humid heat of summer, had rendered all her shoes too tight. After locating a pair of pumps that she had worn in the rain and stretched, she had forced her feet into them and made her way down to the street, where she had found that each and every cab in the city of New York was either in use or off duty. Flying into the door of her office at one minute to eight, she had been confronted by the youngest McGuinn, Peter. Her day had proceeded to worsen steadily from that point, a feat she hadn't believed possible.

One of her clients had been accused of speculating with his clients' money; furthermore, he was suspected of being privy to insider information. She was being subpoenaed.

At that point, all the counselors and partners, junior and senior, had been summoned to a perfectly beastly three-hour meeting to hash the whole mess over, shooting all her plans for the morning straight to hell.

Her day was already an utter loss, she thought, shaking her head with frustration. And it was only eleven-thirty. What else could go wrong?

Courtney's intercom buzzed and she pressed the button to answer her secretary. "Yes, Maggie?"

Maggie's voice, as it came back through the intercom, sounded more than a little shaky. "There's a man out here that says he wants to see you. He won't give me his name. He just said to tell you that he's an investment."

An investment? Lord, no, it couldn't be. . . . She had a sinking feeling it was. The way her day was going so far, it was too much to hope that it wasn't him. "Maggie, this man who says he's an 'investment' . . . tall, dark hair, dark eyes, big?"

"And bearing roses. What should I do with him?" Maggie whispered.

Send him to the World Trade Center and tell him to jump? "I . . ."

"You want me to call security?"

Courtney gave the suggestion serious consideration. She couldn't see Nick, not now. Not ever.

"Ms. Welsch, tell me what to do," Maggie begged.

Courtney covered her mouth with one hand, trying to think. Her brain was hopelessly blocked.

"Ms. Welsch . . . Sir, you can't just go in there . . . Sir? Sir!"

Too late. Nick stood in the doorway of Courtney's office, bigger than life and twice as gorgeous as she remembered him. He looked wonderful, all dressed up in a charcoal gray suit that had to be custom tailored. After the weeks when he still had the cast and was limited to clothing he didn't mind mutilating, it was quite a revelation.

Stunned at his spectacular appearance, Courtney almost stood up behind the desk. Habit, a long-ingrained means of establishing her authority over a situation. This time, with Nick, it would demolish what little control she had. She forced herself to remain seated, even when Maggie wedged her way between Nick and the doorjamb and made a ridiculous attempt to check his progress with her five-two, hundred-and-twenty-pound body.

"Sir, you just can't go barging into Ms. Welsch's office like this. Ms. Welsch, should I call security?"

Courtney's eyes moved from Maggie to Nick and back again. She sighed heavily. Why today? Why her? "No, Maggie, it's okay. I'll take care of it."

Maggie studied her face for a minute, trying to decide whether or not to believe her. She eyed Nick suspiciously, trying to decide if a man in a $700 suit could be an ax murderer. "Fine, Ms. Welsch. I'll be just outside if you need anything."

Courtney knew that translated that meant, "If he turns out to be a nut, yell, and I'll call security and the police."

"Thank you, Maggie."

Easing her way back around Nick, Maggie left them alone, pulling the door closed behind her.

Courtney's head hurt. Violently. Closing her eyes for an instant, she tried to massage away the pain with her fingertips. Finally, sighing deeply, she raised her head to face Nick.

Nick thought Courtney looked absolutely beautiful. The jade green dress she was wearing was perfectly suited to her coloring. It was . . . softer than anything he could remember seeing her wear before, made out of something silky. It made her eyes darker, bringing out blue undertones until they seemed almost indigo.

"Court, have you been as miserable as I've been?"

"Nick, we've been through this already. It won't work."

"Why? Our 'career conflicts,' as you so eloquently phrased it?"

"Nick . . ."

He took several steps into the room, away from the door, and toward her. "Don't say it again. It's ridiculous."

Any other time, she would have stood and slammed her fist on her desk. Now, she stayed where she was. "Are you an ostrich? It is a reason. A damn good one."

"It is not."

"To say nothing of the fact that you lied to me."

"Court . . . At first, it didn't really matter. Later, it was too late to tell you."

"Did you think you were going to get away with lying to me forever? Did you think I wouldn't wonder where you went for weeks at a time?" Courtney's voice dripped with sarcasm.

"Court . . ." Before she knew what was happening, Nick swooped around the desk and crouched next to her chair. Gripping its arms, he swiveled it so that she faced him.

Nick gasped at the same instant that Courtney did.

TWO

"You're pregnant." Every drop of blood rushed out of Nick's face as he choked out the words. He looked, and felt, as if he'd been gut-punched. "But . . . how?"

Courtney couldn't let him discover how vulnerable she was, in spite of the fact that she felt a distinct urge to be ill. In an effort to disguise it, she made her voice deliberately harsher. "Nick, really. How do you think it happened?"

Nick knew exactly how it had happened. By the end of their second day together, he had totally forgotten that Court wasn't his type. He was too entranced to care. Court was bright and funny and delicately beautiful. The urge to wallow in her violet eyes returned and took root in his mind. Her pale skin seemed to make her full lips redder, more lush. He wondered if the rest of her were as fair and creamy as her face. He tried to envision what the body under the bulky wool looked like. He started to imagine what it would feel like moving over and under his own body. By the morning of the third day, idle imaginings had turned into full-blown, vivid fantasies; by the end of the third day, it was spectacular, mind-boggling reality.

"I know that part," Nick snapped angrily as he stood

and stalked around to the front of the desk. "But you said you had a . . ."

"It's never one-hundred percent effective. Poke a hole in it and the percentages go way down."

"When did you find out?"

"About the tear? The day I got back to New York. The baby? In April."

"Before or after I left for Boston?"

Courtney paled and gulped uneasily, lowering her eyes to examine her knuckles.

"Court?" he demanded.

"Before." Guiltily, her voice dropped to a whisper.

"And you let me leave without telling me?"

"I had to, Nick," she pleaded, raising the big violet eyes to meet his.

"Why? Because of my job?"

"Yes." The admission was pained.

"Normally, you're a bright woman, Court, but that's the dumbest thing I've ever heard."

"Dumb?" Her voice rose a full two octaves. "I'm being considered for a junior partnership at the most conservative, low-key investment firm in New York. Do you have any idea what it would do to my chances if anyone found out that the father of my baby is one of the Brawny Buccaneers?"

Courtney recalled precisely when she had made that unwelcome discovery. Jan, who lived next door, had asked her to stay with the two oldest children while she took the third to the emergency room with a fever. Billy, in a profound demonstration that seven-year-old boys' taste did not meet generally accepted social standards, had insisted on watching professional wrestling. Worse yet, he insisted on inflicting his lack of sophistication on innocent bystanders.

"Hey, Aunt Courtney, come see this guy! He's great!"

"Billy, I don't want . . ."

"But, Aunt Courtney . . ." Billy was starting to whine.

Helpless against it, Courtney stepped into the living room to give a split-second's attention to the spectacle before escaping. Her intended meaningless platitudes were replaced by a single stunned gasp.

That tattoo! She almost fell over the back of the sofa when she saw it. An agonizing nausea swept over her as she realized that every inch of that massive body, clad only in boots, snug black wrestling pants, and a mask, was entirely too familiar. Familiar? For heaven's sake, she knew what it tasted like! How much more familiar could you get?

Billy, of course, being seven, was totally oblivious to her horrified reaction. He grinned up at her with innocent exuberance. "Better than Hulk Hogan, huh?"

"That's really good thinking, Court." The body that was better than Hulk Hogan's paced restlessly back and forth in front of her desk. "And it doesn't hurt your chances at all, being an unwed mother?"

"My God, Nick, you make it sound as if I were a fourteen-year-old junior-high student with no means of income. I'm twenty-nine, with a damn good job and an income in the high five figures! I can have a baby without a husband if I want to!" *Now* she could stand up and slap one fist on the desk top. It only detracted slightly from the gesture's effectiveness that she had to haul herself out of the chair.

"You're telling me that no one stopped to wonder how you turned up pregnant with no father for the baby anywhere in sight?" Nick stopped pacing to stare at her incredulously.

What could she tell him? That she'd been fortunate enough to announce her pregnancy hot on the heels of a *Newsweek* feature about biological clocks and women having babies alone because they wanted children before it was too late?

"Who are you telling people is the father?" Nick ranted.

Courtney opened her mouth and closed it again. Several times.

"Well?"

"Artificial insemination," she croaked, knowing he was going to hit the ceiling even as she said it.

"What?"

She flinched violently and he swore expansively.

"Nick . . ."

"Do you mean to tell me that you're telling people that our child was the result of two strangers having unnatural relations with test tubes and syringes?"

It most certainly hadn't been. The last word in the world that would describe their relationship was unnatural. Or clinical. Or impersonal.

They had gotten sick of hot buttered rum on the third day and ordered a bottle of wine instead. After several games of backgammon, betting drinks instead of money, they ordered another bottle. By the time that Julie and Taylor came in from the slopes to meet them for dinner, they were pleasantly stewed and cuddling contentedly in the pit, trying unsuccessfully to make sense out of *The Talisman* despite the fact that they had both read it before.

After dinner and still more wine, they made their way to the bar, where a band was playing for dancing.

"Court, I wish we could ditch these casts for a few hours. I want to dance with you, hold you in my arms . . ."

"You are holding me."

He was. They were slumped together on a banquette at the edge of the room, their casts propped on chairs as they watched the dancers, and Nick's arm pulled her close to his body.

"It's not the same," Nick complained petulantly. "We're just sitting here not moving."

"Would you rather be standing up and moving?"

"I'd rather by lying down and moving," Nick told her softly. "Inside you."

If the deep huskiness in his voice didn't tell Courtney

that he was very serious, the hand that caressed her back enticingly did. In combination, they caused a fleeting shiver that radiated from deep within her.

From the first time she had laid eyes on Nick, she had been attracted to him. Everything about him wreaked havoc on her system. He was so male, so sexy, so disturbingly exciting that she couldn't help indulging fantasies about what Nick would be like as a lover. They'd lingered long after she'd given up the notion as hopeless.

Nick had never given her the slightest indication that he was interested in anything other than friendship. The first day that she had met him, he had made it perfectly clear that he only considered her marginally female. That something had changed the way he thought of her was too much for her to believe.

What had made him change his mind? Could he really want her as much as she had wanted him all along? When had this unexpected development occurred?

Desire warred with doubt. The internal conflict was mirrored on her face and Nick's arm tightened around her reassuringly. "What's wrong, Court?"

"I thought we were friends, Nick."

"We are friends."

"I thought that was all you wanted."

"When I first met you, that was true, honey, but it's changed since then."

"When did it change?"

"It changed, Court. It surprised me." Nick raised one hand to stroke her cheek. "Now I want more, so much more. . . . I want to make love to you."

"When, Nick?" Courtney wanted to believe him so badly she ached. It was just too difficult for her to believe that the man who defined virility wanted her.

"Yesterday."

If he had said the moment he saw her, she would have known he was lying. If he had said he'd just realized it, she would have known he was drunk.

"I dreamed about you last night." Nick's voice dropped to something near a whisper. It was low, mesmerizing, as if he were talking to himself.

"It was gold. . . . Everything was gold, like a Klimt painting, like *The Kiss* or *Danae* . . . that warm, lustrous gold." He wasn't looking at her. He was staring into the distance as if he were seeing the image again as he described it.

"And it smelled like flowers because they were all around us." Courtney couldn't have interrupted him if her life depended on it. She was being drawn into the dream with him, could see it as vividly as he was seeing it again. She could feel it, smell the flowers, as she knew he could.

"And your skin was white, gleaming ivory, just like in the painting, and my skin was so dark against yours. Like day and night, light and shadow . . ." They were both totally oblivious to the room and the music and the people that surrounded them. All that existed for either Nick or Courtney was the sound of Nick's voice and the imagery of his dream.

"We were both naked. Making love to each other . . . exploring every inch of one another with our eyes and our hands and our mouths. It was so slow, so . . . intense, as if it would just go on and on forever. When I touched you, your skin was so smooth . . . like porcelain, except it was soft and warm. . . . And your lips were red and full and they tasted so wonderful. . . . And your hair was like black silk wrapped around me, binding me to you."

Nick's hand had stopped moving on her back, but Courtney felt the caresses from his dream and her body responded to them. Her breasts were taut and a throbbing pulsed deep within her, creating a moist warmth between her thighs.

"And then I was inside of you and we were moving together. You were so tight . . . and I filled you so completely that it was as if . . . we were part of each other. And then you opened your eyes and . . . looked into mine

and . . . they were glowing . . . like burning amethysts
. . . And then we were floating . . . soaring through the
gold . . .'' Nick stopped talking and his chest moved rapidly with his shallow breathing. He raised his head slowly
and turned his head, looking into Courtney's eyes.

The look in his eyes, passion mixed with something
else that she couldn't identify, swept the last shreds of
doubt from Courtney's mind. It was as if she were seeing
into his soul and what she found there called to her, creating a yearning in the deepest part of her that ached to be
fulfilled.

The insistent buzz of the intercom brought them both
back to the present. Courtney depressed the button.
''Yes?''

''Ms. Welsch? Peter McGuinn wants to speak to you.
It's about that business this morning.''

''This minute?'' She knew she wasn't up to dealing
with anything at the moment.

''Before lunch?'' Maggie sounded hesitant, aware that
''before lunch'' meant, in essence, precisely that.

''Tell him I'll be right there.'' Her voice belied the
composure of her words.

''I'll tell him.''

Courtney flipped the switch back. ''I have to go, Nick.''

''We still have to talk.'' The determined note in Nick's
voice brooked no argument.

She nodded reluctantly. ''I know.''

''I'll be back to pick you up this afternoon.''

Courtney got a pained look on her face. ''Not . . . here,
Nick.''

Nick's face mirrored hers. ''I'll be here,'' he insisted,
adding in a cutting voice, ''You don't have to worry. I'll
be discreet. I'll keep my shirt on and no one will recognize
me.''

Damn him anyway! Courtney cursed mentally as she
returned to her office from the meeting with Peter

McGuinn. It had gone every bit as badly as she had feared it would, but her client's legal problems seemed insignificant compared to her problems with Nick. If he didn't stay away from her office, everyone was going to know about his alter ego, and her career was going to be ruined.

The Brawny Buccaneer, indeed! Who could have guessed that gorgeous Nick Trielo was a professional wrestler, of all things. A cartoon character in a cartoon occupation. If you could call it an occupation. The day that she had confronted Nick with her discovery, she'd said plenty worse.

Courtney opened the door and Nick stood in the hall, a basket of violets in his hand and that endearing little-boy grin wide on his face. Appearances were certainly deceiving, which was why no one ever guessed that Clark Kent was Superman, she reminded herself.

"Hi, hon. How was your day? Make lots of money?"

She yanked him into her living room by one elbow. Fortunately, his cast had been removed several days before, or they both would have gone sprawling with their combined weight. She considered breaking his other leg, just for spite.

"Nick, exactly what do you do for a living?"

"Oh-oh." He said it in a high voice, sounding exactly like the Mowgwi in *Gremlins*. His next words were in his own voice, deep, soothing. She vowed not to fall for it, not for a minute. "I gather the jig's up."

"That doesn't begin to cover it," Courtney said ominously. Her eyes flared in warning before she started in. "I think there's something you forgot to tell me, Nick. Or maybe I should call you 'Brawny Buccaneer' or maybe just 'Buck'?"

Nick winced and raked his fingers through his hair uneasily. "How did you find out?"

"Not that it really matters, but it turns out that the little boy next door is one of your biggest fans. I was over there this morning and he insisted on watching wrestling."

"You saw the tattoo and put two and two together."

"I saw you, and came up with four. I work with numbers every day, remember."

"I'm sorry, Court. I should have been the one to tell you."

"First, you should have told me," she snarled. "Then, you should have had the decency to take off for parts unknown."

Nick looked genuinely confused. "And what does that mean?"

"What do you mean, what does that mean? It means, what do you want to be when you grow up?"

"What?"

"It's one thing for you to indulge yourself in this . . . this travesty of an occupation, Nick, but another altogether to inflict it on me without warning."

"Travesty?" Nick repeated incredulously.

"Mockery? Caricature? Farce?"

"I know what travesty means, Court! I went to a good school, too, remember?"

"Childish fantasy? Cartoon?" she continued mercilessly.

"That's enough, Court!"

"I don't think so! Not nearly enough! You made a fool out of me!"

"How did I make a fool out of you?" he demanded.

"By making a damn good attempt at ruining my career, for one!"

"What?"

"Do you have any idea what involvement with the 'Brawny Buccaneer' would do to my career? I'd be laughed right out of a job! How could anyone take me seriously if they found out?"

"This is the most ridiculous thing I ever heard in my life! Court, you're a snob! A first-class, A-number-one snob!"

"I am not! And even if I were, it would be better than being a cartoon character!"

They had flung insults back and forth for several more rounds, she had slung the nearest piece of heavy crystal at him, and Nick had stormed out of her apartment angrily. It was the last time she had seen him, although he had called her again the next day. And the next. And the next—the day the doctor had confirmed her pregnancy. Until she'd had her telephone number changed. Then, the cards and flowers had started coming. She'd forced herself to ignore them all, but there was no way she was going to be able to ignore Nick in-person, live, and standing in front of her.

Damn her anyway! Nick prowled furiously around his hotel room. Courtney never would have told him about the baby, he never would have known, if he hadn't gone to her office to confront her. It was no wonder she'd been avoiding him. She hadn't wanted him to know, not because she'd thought he wouldn't want the baby, but because she hadn't wanted to admit to anyone that he was the father.

He'd never been in prison. He wasn't a bank robber, or a murderer, or anything else really awful. Courtney was ashamed of him for the dumbest reason he'd ever heard. He was an embarrassment. An indiscretion. Lord, what a crock. She was really full of it this time.

It hurt. It hurt to know that the woman who was carrying his baby was telling everyone that the child they'd created together was the product of some laboratory. It hurt like hell to know that he still loved her, in spite of everything.

He wasn't going to let her get away with it.

And he knew how to stop her.

He grinned with determination and picked up the telephone, making the call that solidified his plan to get Courtney back, wondering idly which of the times that they'd made love at the ski lodge they'd made the baby. He hoped it hadn't been the first time, which hadn't quite lived up to the expectations of his dream.

Hadn't quite? Hell, it had been a fiasco. His dream had never taken the strategic, technical reality of two leg casts into consideration, for one thing.

It seemed to take forever to get from the bar to Courtney's room. Her arms weren't strong enough to move her very fast on crutches. It wasn't a leisurely lovers' stroll, either. The hallway was too narrow for them to walk side by side, so he followed after her, feeling slightly ridiculous and enormously frustrated. He wanted Court so badly that he had been in a perpetual state of arousal for the last twenty-four hours. He wanted to slip his arm around her slim waist, pull her tight against his side, and whisper marginally dirty suggestions into her ear while they were on their way to fulfillment of that desire. Instead, he was forced to follow six feet behind her as if they weren't even together. He prayed the awkwardness would end once they got to her room.

It didn't.

Balancing on one leg like two flamingos was not conducive to foreplay. Finally, he suspected out of frustration—perhaps pain because he'd nearly crushed the toes of her good foot when he'd lost his balance—Courtney suggested hesitantly, "I've got an idea."

"I'm sure I'll like it, sweetheart," he answered, dropping a flurry of kisses across her face. "What is it?"

"I have to go . . . uh . . . take care of something anyway . . ."

"Sure." He brushed his mouth across hers.

She pulled her lips away so she could talk. "Nick, let me finish. . . . Is it as much of a production for you to get undressed as it is for me?"

"Probably more. I was right. I do like your idea." He rewarded her with a deep kiss and they very nearly fell over like dominoes. "Hurry."

When Courtney emerged from the bathroom several

minutes later in a short terry robe, he was already under the sheet, wearing nothing but his boyish grin. It had taken considerable effort to get there before she returned.

"You can read my mind," she said, returning his smile.

"If you can read my mind, you'll get over here as soon as you can." He drew back the edge of the sheet nearest to her invitingly. Court was more desirable in terry cloth than most women were in silk and lace, and he felt a warm rush of triumphant pride that she was his. "Come to me, love."

Courtney sat on the edge of the bed and he reached for her hand, turning it to press a kiss into her palm. "Court, darling, I didn't think we'd ever get here."

"Me, neither, Nick. I just kept thinking about everything you said . . . your dream . . . I didn't think it was possible, but I want you more now than I did before."

"Oh, Court . . . me, too. I want you so much, sweetheart." Looping his arms around her waist, he pulled her to him, finding the sweetness of her mouth.

Her lips were soft and warm and moist, making the most tantalizing promises and then fulfilling them. They were tender and passionate and generous and greedy, all at the same time. He thought he could spend the rest of his life exploring the full range of Court's kisses. Breaching the portal of her lips, his tongue delved into her mouth, mingling their tastes, their breaths intimately.

Even through the plush terry of her robe, he could feel her nipples, full with anticipation for him. A surge of desire coursed through his veins, growing stronger with each passing moment. Court felt it, too. He knew it, felt the tremor shake her, felt her hands move between them to work loose the tie of her robe. The front fell open and her bare breasts rubbed against his chest, hard peaks tormenting his ribs. Each breath was an agonizing struggle. His heart pounded with an intensity that insisted that each beat would be its last. His manhood, hard and throbbing, demanded release. It was too soon . . . too soon, he told himself. If he didn't get control of himself, it was all going to be over before it started.

"Court . . . love," he murmured against her mouth as he eased their bodies apart. "Please . . . I want to see you . . . let me . . ." He pushed the robe from her shoulders to the floor.

She was exquisite. Her skin was so creamy, so white, so like his fantasies. Like . . . porcelain. He touched the curve of her breast tentatively, as if she were as fragile as she appeared. It was so soft and warm. Not porcelain. Most definitely not porcelain. Every inch of Court was woman, female beyond imagination. Pink and white and his . . . all his.

"Perfect . . . so perfect . . ." He brushed one nipple with his thumb and watched, mesmerized, as it swelled under his touch. Bending his head, he found the rosy bud with his mouth and fondled it with his lips and teeth and tongue.

"Nick . . . darling Nick . . ." Court whispered as she nibbled at the rim of his ear, her words setting up a series of vibrations that reverberated throughout his body, growing stronger with each echo. "Love me . . . oh, please love me . . ."

"Oh, Court, love . . ." His arms tightened around her waist and he fell back, her body dragging across his as he took her mouth again hungrily. His tongue plunged inside, seeking her sweetness, her essence . . .

Courtney's hand burrowed under the sheet and found his hardness. Her fingers curled to grasp him and his hand shot down to catch her wrist reflexively. "No . . . no, sweetheart . . ."

"Nick . . ."

"Please don't . . ." he choked, loosening his grip on her wrist as her arm retreated from its loving assault. "If you touch me . . . I won't be able to hold back . . ."

"Then don't wait . . . Nick, darling, please . . . I want you . . . now." Taking his hand, she guided it to the warm moist place between her thighs. "I'm ready . . . so ready for you, Nick . . ."

"Oh, Court . . . Court . . ." His fingers tunneled through the black curls at her temples and he kissed her fiercely as he rolled them both to move his body over hers.

"Oh, Nick!" Through the haze of passion, he heard the frantic note in her voice alerting him to the fact that something was very wrong.

An instant later, he realized what it was when he felt the edge of the mattress at the top of his thigh, above his cast. "Oh, God, no! Not now!" Defenseless against the combined forces of gravity, inertia, and fifty pounds of plaster, he fell, striking the floor with a sickening thud and a flash of pain that shot out from his hip.

More frustrated than hurt, he groaned miserably, slamming his fist against the carpeting.

"Nick? Are you hurt, darling?"

He took a deep breath and let it out slowly. "Only my dignity."

"Are you sure?" Her concerned face peered over the edge of the bed at him.

"Positive." He grinned up at her. "Come on down and I'll prove it."

No, he certainly didn't want any child of his conceived on the floor of a hotel room.

THREE

Each day before she left her office, Courtney tried to plow through the heap that covered her desk in an effort to bring some semblance of order to the chaos. The ritual gave her one last chance to determine if there was anything important she had forgotten, helped her to make tentative plans for the following day, and allowed her to weed out the real trash and get rid of it. Her biggest problem always was deciding what to do with things that didn't seem to fit into any of the three categories.

Courtney leaned back in her chair and stared at the piece of paper with the telephone number written on it. No name, no company, no identification of any kind. It was her handwriting, but she didn't recall writing it. Her options were simple: call the number and see who answered the telephone, pitch it into the trash, or throw it back into the pile and see if it made any sense the next time she found it. She was rescued from making the momentous decision by the buzz of her intercom.

When she answered it, Maggie hissed, "Courtney, he's back!" in a panicky voice. "What should I do?"

Nick. Lord, in all the confusion, she'd forgotten about him. How, she wasn't sure.

"Should I call security?"

And tell them what? Courtney asked herself silently. Aloud, she answered, "I'm expecting Mr. Trielo, Maggie. Tell him I'll be through in a few minutes."

If there had been another exit from her office, Courtney would have used it. Escape sounded infinitely preferable to facing Nick. For that matter, root canal sounded preferable to facing Nick.

It had been difficult enough to maintain her resolve when Nick had been safely out of town and out of sight, her communication with him limited to those infernal cards and flowers. Then, she could come close to believing it when she told herself that letting go of Nick was the only viable, reasonable solution for her to make if she wanted to keep her career. With Nick around, she knew that it was going to be impossible for her to think clearly, keep reality in focus. And if he touched her—Lord, she was a goner. Inside of thirty seconds, he'd have her convinced that professional wrestling was a perfectly respectable occupation for an adult.

Her intercom buzzed frantically several times, simultaneously with the opening of her office door. She didn't need to look up to know who was there.

"Nick, really . . . if you don't stop barging in here, Maggie's going to call security."

"Or the police," he added, laughing lightly as if he'd forgotten their argument that morning. "What did you tell that woman about me? She looks at me as if I were some sort of fiend."

"I didn't tell her anything about you." Courtney replied with a cold disinterest in her voice. It couldn't have said more if she'd actually yawned.

"Nothing?" A crestfallen expression replaced the amusement.

"Nothing," Courtney repeated firmly. Nick looked like a kicked puppy and she steeled herself against her inclination to apologize, reminding herself that she had already made the only possible decision. "She never heard your name before this morning. And she still doesn't know why it should mean anything."

Fighting back the hurt, Nick reminded himself that he was in control of the situation. "Court, you can deny it all you want, but it's not going to change a thing."

"And what does that mean?"

"I'm the father of that baby, Court." He pointed at her stomach. "That's my child, too."

The abrupt change in his voice, the emergence of the familiar self-assurance, set off an alarm in Courtney's mind. With a swift intake of air, she paled several shades. "What are you saying, Nick?" she asked hesitantly.

"Don't look so stricken, Court. I'm not going to fight for custody, if that's what you're afraid of."

"What do you want, then?"

Nick dropped into a chair and stretched out his long legs in front of him as if he were settling in for the duration. "I want to talk."

His words were calm, measured, and confident. They gave Courtney chills.

Reining in her sudden rush of panic, Courtney crossed her arms beneath her breasts and settled into her chair with a carefully-enforced and tenuously-held facade of indifference. "So talk."

"I have some rights where this baby is concerned. And I intend to exercise them. I have no intention of letting my child grow up without knowing his father." He dug into the side pocket of his jacket, withdrew several sheets from a legal pad, and unfolded them. "After I left here this morning, I spoke with my lawyer."

Courtney gritted her teeth with irritation. If he didn't stop talking in that maddeningly matter-of-fact way of his, she was going to leap across the desk and throttle him.

Nick separated the papers into two sections, leaned forward, laid one heap in front of Courtney, and leaned back in his chair without saying a word.

Courtney flipped through the pages quickly, giving them only the most cursory glance before she looked up at Nick. "Demands?"

Nick suppressed a grin of satisfaction and gave himself a mental pat on the back. He knew he had Court right where he wanted her. Bringing one ankle up to rest casually on the other knee, he laid the papers on his lap and said, "Essentially, I want all the rights and privileges of any father. Nothing I'm asking for is outrageous, by anyone's standards, except maybe yours." He glanced down at the paper and started in a business-like manner. "First, visitation rights. Mark—Mark Graham, he's my lawyer— tells me that one night during the week, every other weekend, and a month in the summer is reasonable. I wanted to ask for more, but he says that your lawyer would tell me to go jump off a cliff."

He paused long enough to study Courtney's expression. She looked shell-shocked. "Second," he continued serenely, "approval of major decisions involving the child. Schools, camps, non-emergency medical care, place of residence . . ."

"What?" Courtney interrupted angrily, rising halfway out of her seat.

"Don't panic, Court," he explained in a tone that suggested he thought he was talking to a two year old. "All that means is that I don't want you taking the baby and moving to Alaska without telling me."

She eyed him suspiciously as she lowered herself back into her chair. "Oh."

"It's all itemized here, so I won't go into it. The gist of it is that I want some say in how the child's going to be raised," he added. "Third, child support . . ."

"I don't want your money, Nick."

"So put it in a trust fund for the kid," he suggested levelly. "Fourth, I want the baby to have my name . . ."

"What?" she asked again, feeling more than a little foolish to keep asking the same stupid question. Why that condition had taken her by surprise, she didn't know. If Nick were eagerly anticipating fatherhood—which he obviously was—it was an understandable request. It sure wreaked havoc with her artificial insemination story, though.

"We can discuss hyphenating names for the baby," Nick continued calmly, as if he didn't know what he'd just done to her interesting piece of fiction. "It's a bit of a mouthful for a baby, but it's workable."

He paused as he leafed through to the last page on his lap. He was getting to the real killers, the ones that would bring her to her feet screaming for blood. His. "Fifth, I want to be present at the child's birth."

"I don't want you there."

"Forget it, Court. I want to be there. I helped to make that baby and I want to help with his birth."

"I have a partner already."

"Who?"

"Julie."

"Good. She won't object to my taking her place." He'd had a sudden pang of terror that she'd asked her mother or someone else who would object.

"I want Julie there."

"It's my place, not Julie's, and you know it. Besides, and here's the last demand, I intend to participate fully in your pregnancy."

"Meaning?" Courtney asked antagonistically.

"Meaning," Nick answered confidently, "I'm moving in with you until the baby's born."

Courtney gaped at him incredulously, unable to summon words as she digested Nick's last demand.

"It shouldn't be too much of an imposition for you," Nick continued flatly. "That is a two-bedroom apartment."

She blinked rapidly several times in an effort to collect herself. It helped, if only a little bit. At last she found her voice, along with a sudden rush of anger. "You want . . .

to move in with me? Just like that? Don't I get any say in this?"

"No."

How could he be so . . . calm about this? So sure of himself . . . and her? "I've already started the renovations on the spare room."

He shrugged lazily. "I can live with paint fumes."

"I sold the bedroom suite to make room for the baby's furniture. Surely you don't expect to sleep in the crib. I don't think you'll fit." She eyed his six-three, two-fifty frame meaningfully.

"I'll sleep on the sofa."

"I won't let you do this to me."

"Yes, you will."

"You can't make me." She stuck out her jaw stubbornly.

"If you don't agree to this, Court, I'll call Richard Martelli and give him the scoop that the Brawny Buccaneer is going to become a father."

Courtney closed her eyes against the mental picture. Within twenty-four hours, everyone on the subway would be able to read her whole life story on one of the world's sleaziest newspapers—not that it really deserved the title.

Nick didn't help her struggle against the images. "Can't you just see the headline, Court? BUCCANEER AND STOCK ANALYST AWAIT BIRTH OF LOVE CHILD."

She could see it. All too vividly. It wasn't a pretty picture.

"You wouldn't, Nick."

"Only if you don't cooperate with me, Court. Give me access to my baby."

"That's blackmail," she accused.

He broke into a broad grin. "I know."

She opened her mouth to speak, thought better of it, and closed it again.

"You won't marry me, Court. I can't do anything to change that. But I'm not letting you cheat me out of my child."

* * *

Numbed by the magnitude of Nick's demands, Courtney was docile and silent as he led her out of her office, retrieved his luggage from the now—deserted reception room, and installed them both in a cab. She neither looked at him nor spoke as the vehicle wended its slow way through the rush-hour traffic toward her apartment building, a monument to Art Deco overlooking Central Park, where Nick helped her from the cab and propelled her through the lobby and into the elevator.

As the door slid closed behind them, Courtney's eyes skittered sideways, peering at Nick through the filter of her lashes. The big hand clenched around the handle of his suitcase was white-knuckled. In fact, every muscle in his body was tense with anger. His face was stony, grim, bearing only a superficial physical resemblance to the man that, in spite of everything, she still loved. If she didn't know better, she'd think that some stranger had taken possession of Nick's body. A stranger that didn't like her very much.

Gone was the charming, loving Nick who had begged her to marry him every day for the last three months; he had vanished the instant that Nick had learned about the baby. The new Nick had made it apparent that his only concern now was the baby. The baby was the only thing he had talked about, his only reason for returning to her office that afternoon, his only motive for moving into her apartment.

Not only did Nick not love her anymore, but Courtney seriously suspected that he hated her. The realization raised contradictory emotions in her, hurting her deeply at the same time that it caused an immense wave of relief to wash over her.

For weeks, Nick's inevitable reappearance had hung over her head, threatening her sanity. She had no self-control around him—she never had—and she had just known that one of his smoldering looks or one touch of his hand would be enough to make her forget the devastating effect he would have on her career. For that matter, with the least effort, he could make her forget that she had a career. But if Nick didn't love her anymore, didn't want her anymore, resisting him wasn't going to be a problem.

Nick was confused. He hadn't expected such meek compliance from Courtney. He'd expected her to scream, carry on, insult him, just the way she had done when she had thrown him out of her life fifteen weeks earlier. Perhaps he'd gone a bit too far, but he was a desperate man. He wasn't going to let Court get away from him again. Letting her put up this wall between them had been a mistake, one he was determined to correct. Moving into her apartment, ostensibly "to participate in the pregnancy," was a stroke of genius, even if he did say so himself. If he could live with her, take care of her, show her he loved her in a hundred little everyday ways, he knew he could, in time, overcome her objections. He wanted Court back every bit as much as he wanted the baby—more—but he couldn't let her know that. Not yet.

The elevator opened and they walked silently out and down the hall to Courtney's apartment. She dug her keys out of her purse and, after a brief battle of wills for their possession, opened the door and walked inside.

Nick was horrified by the sight that met him. The living room looked as if a bomb had gone off. There were books, magazines, newspapers, clothing, and shoes everywhere. Gasping in horror, he dropped his suitcase just inside the door and charged across the room to the telephone, snatching up the receiver.

Courtney, still standing in the open door, just stared at him. "What are you doing?"

"Calling the police!" he snapped, the receiver in his hand. "Why are you just standing there? Is anything missing?"

"What?"

"You're being awfully calm for someone whose apartment's been ransacked!" Hanging up the telephone, he crossed the room again to take her arm. "It's probably shock. Come on, you ought to sit down."

"What?" she repeated in astonishment.

Nick looked at her face, at the room, and back at her face again. "This apartment hasn't been ransacked?"

Courtney shook her head slowly and tried to stifle the laugh she felt building inside her. "No."

"What happened?" he demanded.

"Carmelita quit."

"Carmelita?"

"My cleaning lady."

"I thought your cleaning lady's name was Molly or Mary or Millie or something like that."

"It was Maude. And she was three cleaning ladies ago. She quit." Courtney shrugged indifferently. "They all quit."

"There's no need to ask why," Nick said sharply. "This place looks like Dresden after the war."

"Carmelita made it quite clear in two languages that a twice-a-week cleaning lady didn't begin to cover what I need."

"She's right. Don't worry about it. I'll take care of it."

"You're going to hire my new cleaning lady? Good. I haven't had the time to do any interviewing."

"I'm not going to do any interviewing," Nick said firmly. "I mean, I'll take care of it."

"You're going to clean for me?"

"Sure." He shrugged confidently. "I'll have plenty of time. I'll only be going to the gym for a couple of hours every day."

"You're going to clean for me?" Courtney repeated incredulously.

"And I won't be doing anything that'll take me away for more than overnight until the baby's born," he added. It was a spur-of-the-moment decision and he hadn't told

Jake yet. His manager was going to have fits when he told him . . . so let him, he decided. Court and the baby were more important to him right now. "Everything between Boston and D.C.'s an easy run, either by train or commuter flight."

"Don't expect me to argue with you. If you want to clean, be my guest." She turned toward the bedroom. "I have to go and change clothes."

"Court?"

She turned back. "Yes, Nick?"

"When did Carmelita quit?"

"Last Monday." She turned and continued into the bedroom.

Nine days ago? Nick looked down at the pair of shoes that Courtney had discarded just inside the door and wondered exactly what he'd gotten himself into.

That suspicion echoed in his mind as he walked into the kitchen. Court was, without a doubt, one of the most supremely undomestic women he had ever known. The room surpassed anything he had ever seen, even living with Steve, whom he had always thought set world standards for squalor.

The garbage can was full, and two tied-off bags sat next to it. He shuddered to think of the effort it had taken to accumulate that much trash in an apartment with a garbage disposal and trash chutes in the halls. Upon closer inspection, all the trash appeared to be paper—the carcasses of TV dinners and bags and boxes from every kind of take-out between her office and her apartment. He grimaced and wondered when she'd had her last decent meal.

The interior of her refrigerator confirmed his worst fears. Little goldfish boxes from the Chinese. The foil-and-plastic containers from the nearby gourmet-to-go. A flat pizza box. A box of HoHos. A jug of spring water. The freezer was more of the same. It looked like the frozen-food department at Waldbaum's. Every TV dinner and frozen entree known to man or woman. Four kinds of ice cream. A bag of Milky Ways. And a plastic bag containing six pairs of pantyhose.

At least she'd been eating off real dishes. The dishwasher hadn't been run, or even loaded, since Carmelita had wisely fled for the hills. If there was a clean dish in her apartment, he didn't know where to start looking for it. He wasn't sure he'd recognize it if he found it.

The whole room was like something out of a bad horror movie, *The Invasion of the Kitchen Monsters*. He got a mental picture of the promotional ads. What lurks in the deepest recesses under the sink? What lives in the refrigerator? Only the Shadow knows. . . . Uneasily, his eyes kept roving, as if he were waiting for something to spring at him.

Even as Nick entertained himself with visions of being attacked by the somewhat ripe remains of marinated scallops and chives, he contemplated his most immediate problem—dinner. It was apparent to him that there wasn't enough real food in the apartment to nourish roaches.

He considered the possible consequences of a trip to the grocery store. If he left the apartment before he had his own key, Court might lock him out. If he took her key with him, she might call a locksmith before he returned. It was even within the realm of possibility that she might go so far as to move while he was gone.

"Nick?"

The sound of Courtney's voice was sufficient to interrupt his reverie. "Yes, Court?"

"I have to go out."

"Already? You haven't eaten yet. Is there anything . . ." He broke off in mid-sentence when he turned around and faced Courtney. He blinked, several times, at the sight. It was somewhere between bizarre and ludicrous.

"What are you staring at?"

Nick blinked again, as if it would make the picture

clearer—or make it go away. He couldn't speak. He'd never seen a pregnant woman in a leotard before.

"I have an exercise class," Courtney explained levelly.

It made sense; it just didn't add up in his brain. "Exercise?" he repeated weakly.

"Exercise. You know, exercise." She brought her hands above her head and back to her sides again in a half-hearted demonstration of a jumping jack.

To the best of his knowledge, Court had never done anything more strenuous and athletic than putting on sweats and sneakers to go out for the Sunday *Times*. "You've never exercised before."

Courtney smiled grimly. "Regular exercise during pregnancy makes natural childbirth easier."

He frowned at her. "Regular meals help, too."

She shrugged. "I'll grab something when I get back. If I eat before class, it upsets my stomach."

He'd concede that point to her. If eating later was more comfortable for her, so be it. But he wasn't going to let her eat that trash that was in her refrigerator. "I'll need your keys."

"What for?" she asked suspiciously.

"I'm going to the grocery store and get some real food for you."

"I have real food." Her voice was laced with disgust as she opened the freezer to show him.

"No, Court. Real food. That stuff's just full of salt and preservatives. There aren't enough nutrients in there to keep a plant alive."

Courtney gritted her teeth at him. He wasn't here ten minutes, and he was trying to take over already. What was he going to be like in four months?

"The keys, Court. How long will you be?"

"About two hours, I guess. Counting cab time."

"All right. That gives me plenty of time." On his way into the living room, he hooked the keys out her fingers.

"When you get back from class, we'll discuss your schedule."

Nick watched Court storm out of the apartment, slamming the door behind her. At last, he allowed himself a wry smile. She was furious, absolutely livid. But she hadn't argued with him. She had handed over the keys and agreed, implicitly, anyway, to eat the meal that he made her when she came back. Before he went to the store, though, he had to call Jake. On second thought, it would be easier to start with Steve. Pulling the schedule from his hip pocket, he figured out where Steve was now and reached for the telephone.

" 'Discuss my schedule,' indeed!" Courtney muttered to herself as she strode angrily out the front of the building, regretting that the glass and steel doors didn't close with a good, solid, satisfying slam. She knew she needed to find a cab to take her down to her exercise class in the Village, but at the moment finding a telephone so that she could talk to Julie was more critical. After thinking about it for a moment, she recalled that there was one in front of the pharmacy in the next block. Purposefully, she set off in that direction.

The telephone rang twelve times. Nick was almost ready to hang up when it stopped abruptly. The greeting that carried through the wires to his ear was more of a snarl. "Yes?"

"Steve?"

"Nicky, is that you?" The voice was decidedly friendlier than it had been at first. "Where are you?"

"New York."

"I know that. What I mean is, are you still at the hotel?"

"I'm staying at Court's . . ." he began.

"Great! I told you she'd come around if you went and talked to her."

"She didn't. And isn't. She's barely speaking to me."

"But, you're . . ."

"Sleeping on the sofa," Nick completed for him.

"Oh." Although the next words were muffled, Nick still heard them. "Hey, babe, could you throw me a towel?" Steve spoke into the telephone again. "What . . ."

"Hey, Steve, I'm sorry . . . you're busy. I'll call you back later . . ."

"It's okay. I was in the shower."

"Not alone."

"I said, it's okay. You sound like this is important."

Nick heard a squeal of outrage. Obviously, Steve's companion was bright enough to infer that she wasn't.

"Hey, babe, where you going?" Steve forgot to cover the mouthpiece and the argument carried clearly over the lines.

"I'm leaving. Talk to your friend . . ."

"Don't leave . . ."

"Pop quiz . . . one question. What's my first name?" Steve hesitated too long before answering. "Elaine?"

"Damn you . . . it's Lorraine! Goodbye!" The door slammed behind her.

"Julie, you won't believe what he's done now!" Courtney didn't even wait for her friend to greet her after answering the telephone; the second it stopped ringing, she started right in. "He's gone too far this time, and I won't stand for it!"

"Courtney, calm down." Taylor sounded just as placid and levelheaded as he always did. Nothing ever excited or frustrated him, which was probably why he was a lawyer.

"I am calm, Taylor!" she lied.

"Your nose is going to grow faster than your stomach, at the rate you're going."

"Is Julie there?" she snapped, irritated with her best friend's husband. His analytical nature was giving her a headache. "Put her on the phone."

"She has group tonight."

"Oh. Damn!" Her current humor demanded high emotion, of which Taylor was incapable. Julie, on the other hand, was an old pro at it, which was probably why she was a therapist.

Taylor sighed wearily, well aware that any hopes he'd had of getting a lot of work done while Julie was out had just flown out the window. He couldn't just leave her out there. "Where are you, Courtney?"

She told him.

"Put your butt in a cab and get over here."

"I can't! I have exercise class. . . ."

"This is more important, kiddo. You're too upset to exercise, anyway. Just come on over and tell me what he's done now."

"Oh . . . damn, she's gone." Steve's sigh sounded disappointed but resigned, hardly devastated. The impression was validated by the way his attention immediately returned to Nick. "Hey, buddy, you still there?"

"Yeah. Steve, I'm sorry . . . I didn't mean to run off your lady. . . ."

"Trust me, Nicky, she wasn't a lady." Steve's shrug was almost audible, and Nick had a reasonably descriptive mental image of the woman who had just left Steve's room. He was his best friend, but his taste in women was questionable at best. "No great loss." The pitiful thing was that it was probably true. "I'm sure you didn't call just to drag me out of the shower, though. . . . What's going on there? You said Court's not speaking to you, but you're staying at her apartment . . ."

"Barely speaking . . ." Nick corrected before remembering that he hadn't called to get advice or sympathy from Steve. What he'd called for was to check out the current situation and see if it were possible for him to take the time to be with Court. "So, did you find a temporary partner?"

"Great news! Well, not great, depending on your perspective. . . . Mike Warren hurt his back and he's out of commission for a few weeks. Greg says he'll work with me until you come back. . . ." Steve's voice faded off. "How long do you think you'll be gone?"

"October."

"October?" Steve repeated.

"Second week, I think. Court's pregnant."

FOUR

When Courtney stumbled out of the cab, Taylor was waiting for her in the lobby. At once, it became apparent to him that it was going to be a long evening, filled with *sturm* and *drang*. And when Julie got home, they'd have to start all over again. With a brisk efficiency honed by years of dealing with Julie and Courtney's most emotional crises, he hustled her into the building and up to the apartment before she could create a public scene. Once there, he settled her into a corner of the sofa with a glass of lemonade.

"Now, Courtney," Taylor began in the voice that always reassured his clients. "Calm down. It can't be that bad." Her eyes rolled wildly and he added, "Can it?"

She gulped and nodded.

The legal mind churned and spat out the reason for her distress. "Nick found out about the baby? You knew he would, didn't you? Somehow or other, he was going to hear about it eventually."

"But . . . he came to my office this morning . . ."

Taylor closed his eyes and took a deep, restorative breath. He didn't like the sounds of it already. The concept of Nick Trielo in the conservative offices of the brothers

McGuinn was disturbing at best. "Did he . . . cause trouble?"

"He didn't bare his chest and let out his famous whoop, if that's what you mean."

Taylor thanked heaven for small favors. "Exactly what did he do?"

"He went and saw a lawyer this afternoon . . ."

"He doesn't want custody, does he?" Taylor interrupted, his voice straining with hard-won control.

Courtney shook her head and Taylor sighed in relief. "But he does want to be a father."

"Pregnant?" Steve echoed incredulously. "Hey, Nicky, I'm sorry . . ."

"I'm not."

"You're not?" Steve couldn't understand it. To his way of thinking, it was bad news.

"Steve, I'm thrilled about it!"

"You are?" If a woman told him that he was going to be a father, "thrilled" wouldn't be his first response.

"I want to lay off the touring until the baby's born . . . just keep in shape and do some workouts and a few bouts. I have to talk to Jake about it, but I don't want to do anything longer than overnight for a while."

"Did you two get married?"

Nick grimaced. It was what he was hoping for eventually, but talking about it as a foregone conclusion was tempting fate. "Steve, she's hardly speaking to me."

"But you're staying with her."

"Only because I threatened to go and talk to Richard Martelli if she wouldn't cooperate with me."

"So what did he do that's got you so worked up? Ask you to marry him? He's been doing that all along." It had to be something worse, Taylor knew, but Courtney had to tell him what it was. He refused to play guessing games with her. "Back up and start at the beginning."

She did. Courtney related Nick's two visits to her office and his list of demands. "He can't do this, can he?"

It was a rhetorical question, but, as usual, Taylor took it literally. The look on his face was thoughtful as he considered everything she had said. Finally, he spoke. "Courtney, everything Nick's asked for is well within reason. More importantly, it's well within the law. If you fight him, he might ask for a lot more. And get it."

"But he's moved in with me!" Courtney raged, slamming her fist on the arm of the sofa.

"Moved in?" It didn't make sense. The last time he'd looked, there was a lock on Courtney's door. Nick could never have gotten into her apartment if she hadn't let him in.

"He says if I don't let him live with me until the baby's born, he'll go and tell Richard Martelli that he's going to be a father!"

"Martelli? That slime bucket? Why would anyone talk to him? More importantly, why would you talk to him?"

"Blackmail," Nick said levelly.

"What?" Steve secretly harbored suspicions that his best friend had gone over the deep end.

"You know how embarrassed Court is about the wrestling. Get a picture in your mind of how she'd react to people reading about our relationship on the front page of that rag."

"Why'd you do that, Nick? All it'll do is make her mad."

"It already did." Nick grinned wickedly. "But it also gives me leverage. She won't just throw me out of here now."

"She'll hate you, Nick."

"Right now, I'm sure she does," Nick confirmed. He didn't have a doubt in the world about that. "But I love her, and I think she still loves me. If I didn't, I wouldn't have done it."

Steve's groan was eloquent; the curse that followed it wasn't. "Nick . . ."

"When I told her I intended to give her child support, she told me to shove the money."

"Nick, a woman with her income doesn't need the money."

"If she didn't love me, she would have taken it," Nick argued with conviction.

Steve conceded that it made sense, in a peculiar sort of way.

"Isn't there anything that I can do?" Courtney demanded furiously.

"Not as far as I can tell . . . except put clean sheets in the spare room." Taylor eyed Courtney speculatively. "Unless you'd enjoy having your dirty linen aired in the subway."

"I don't have a spare room anymore! I've already started the renovations!"

Taylor had known Courtney long enough to recognize that a sudden obsession with minutiae generally masked a real reluctance to deal with more important issues.

"Can't I stop him?"

"From announcing that he's going to be a father? Be realistic, Courtney."

"From moving in with me?"

That was the crux of it, Taylor told himself. She didn't want Nick living with her. And it wasn't because she hated him. It was because it was easier to convince herself that she hated Nick when he wasn't there.

"He's only been there since this afternoon and he's taking over already!" Courtney raged, slamming her glass on the coffee table. "He wants to know where I'm going, when I'll be back! Do you know what he's doing right now? Grocery shopping!"

Taylor suppressed a smile of masculine sympathy. Nick wanted to take care of Courtney. It was apparent that he

still loved her, in spite of the lousy way she treated him.
And he intended to win her back.

"But why'd you move in with her, for God's sake?"

"I can't think of a better place to be while I convince
her that I still love her." When Steve didn't answer, Nick
added, "It's perfect, don't you see? I'll be here all the
time. I can show her, take care of her . . . and Lord
knows she needs it."

"Not to throw a monkey wrench in your plans, but I
think Courtney Welsch is perfectly capable of taking care
of herself."

"You'd never know it by this apartment. Remember the
way our place in college looked?"

"Yes." Nick could almost hear the cringe.

"It's worse. She's had three cleaning ladies quit since
we went on tour. And I don't know when she had her last
decent meal. She needs someone to take care of her."

"I'm sure she wouldn't admit that."

"Of course not. And I wouldn't be the one to try and
tell her that, either."

"If you won't admit why you're doing this, what did
you tell her?"

"I told her I want to participate in the pregnancy. I
really do, so I wasn't lying to her. I've missed so much
of it already."

"I can't see Courtney quietly letting you do this."

"She didn't. That's the beauty of threatening her with
Martelli. Even if she's not happy with it right now, she's
going to have to live with it. And that'll give me time to
convince her that I'm not going to let her get away again."

"He can't treat me this way!" Courtney railed. "It's
as if he thinks I don't have a mind of my own! A right
to a life of my own!"

"That baby is his, too, Courtney. He's got rights, too.
You can't just pretend he doesn't exist."

As if she could pretend that a man that size, living in her apartment, didn't exist.

"He has every right to make the announcement that he's going to be a father to anyone he wants to tell." Although every word Taylor said was that of a friend, they wore the guise of legal advice. He knew that, at the moment, it was all that she would accept.

"Even Richard Martelli?"

"Even Richard Martelli. You have no legal recourse because he wouldn't be lying." It was true, but his real purpose in saying it was to make amends for the way he had stonewalled Nick for the last few months. Obviously, the guy deserved a little help.

"But what can I do?" Courtney wailed miserably. She needed helpful, concrete advice, not confirmation that there was nothing she could do.

"Not a damn thing," Taylor answered, knowing full well that it wasn't what she wanted to hear. "If you don't want everyone in the United States to know about you and Nick, and if letting him play doting father-to-be will satisfy him, that's precisely what you'll have to do."

Propping his hips against the edge of the counter and crossing his arms over his chest, Nick surveyed the newly-cleaned kitchen and smiled with satisfaction. He could scarcely believe that this was the same disaster of a room that he had entered earlier that evening; it certainly wasn't recognizable as such.

For one thing, he could see the floor. Before he'd begun, its existence had been a matter of faith rather than proven fact. Finding it had filled him with admiration for Carmelita's astuteness. She had known precisely what she was doing when she had walked out the door. If he hadn't wanted Court back so badly, he would have done the same.

Briefly, he was grateful that no one was here to see him playing *hausfrau* because it would have wreaked havoc with his image. He stifled the thought, reminding himself that "image" was what had caused all the trouble between himself and Court in the first place. If he had to scrub a few floors and clean a few toilets to negate that ridiculous macho image that she objected to, it wouldn't kill him.

He'd even made dinner. A great meal, since he was being honest with himself. All right, so it had taken a half-dozen excruciatingly humiliating phone calls to his sister to accomplish it. Gina had thought the concept of her brother in the kitchen was hysterical—so hilarious that he'd vowed that hell would freeze over before he called her again; he had three other sisters, after all. And there was always Selena.

And now the kitchen was habitable. Dinner was ready. There were clean dishes to serve it on. All that was missing was Court.

Nick glanced up at the kitchen clock and started pacing. She'd been gone far longer than he'd expected. Somehow, a couple of hours had turned into five. It was eleven o'clock, he hadn't the slightest idea where Courtney was, and it worried him. More than that, it terrified him. He thought about the weeks he'd been away and hadn't known where Court was. Although it hadn't bothered him at the time, it did now. Horrible visions of Court being hit by a cab, a bus, a truck, skittered about on the edge of his consciousness. He banished them, only to have them replaced by others of Courtney being mugged, kidnapped, or God only knew what else. . . .

Through sheer willpower, he suppressed the fears that assaulted him. He assured himself that the most probable reason for her absence was that she was avoiding him. He wondered if she were making an intentional effort to drive him crazy, or if it only happened to be an incidental side effect of this little stunt. The thought made him so angry that he wanted to wring her neck.

The telephone rang and Nick jumped, startled by the sound. He raced into the living room and stared at it, mesmerized by the sound of the bell, too petrified to pick it up. What if it was the police? The hospital? Or, God forbid, the morgue?

He was being morbid, he told himself firmly. He ordered himself to stop this nonsense at once as he reached for the receiver and picked it up. "Hello?" he asked tentatively.

"Nick?" a man's voice answered.

Who knew where he was? Only Steve and Jake, and it wasn't either of them.

"This is Taylor Killian. Julie's husband?" the caller identified himself.

Nick heaved a sigh of relief. If Taylor knew that he was in Courtney's apartment, it meant . . . "Please tell me Court's with you," he begged.

"She's here," Taylor assured him. "Has been since about six-thirty. You've got her pretty worked up, Nick."

"She's all right, though, isn't she?"

"She's fine. I thought I should give you a call and let you know."

"Thanks, Taylor. You can't imagine how much I needed to hear you say that."

"I think I have a good idea of how much." His own relationship with Julie had had its moments. "Neither Julie nor Courtney knows I'm calling you, by the way. I didn't tell them because I didn't think they'd appreciate me consorting with the enemy."

"The enemy? Is that what I am?"

"That's what they think you are at the moment. And what they think is a lot more important than what's true."

"Damn." Nick lowered his head and shook it slowly. "I never wanted to be her enemy."

"I know, Nick. But with Courtney being stubborn and Julie encouraging her . . ." Taylor's voice trailed off. It wasn't necessary for him to complete the thought.

"What can I do, Taylor?" Nick pleaded.

"Exactly what you are doing. Congratulations, Nick. Moving in with Courtney was sheer genius."

"But now I'm here and she's there."

"Leave her here for tonight. Once she has a chance to calm down, she'll see reason and come back."

"But she hasn't seen reason in nearly four months, Taylor," Nick argued.

"But now you're in her apartment. And she certainly can't go to work tomorrow in a leotard and sweatpants. You'll see her in the morning."

Nick had needed the conversation with Taylor more than he had known. In addition to letting him know that Court was safe, it was good for him to hear from someone who thought he was doing the right thing for all the right reasons.

Taylor had seen right through his pretense that he was more concerned with the baby than with Court. It was significant that Taylor had not voiced that knowledge to Court and, apparently, had no intention of doing so. Nick respected Taylor's opinion. In addition to being sharp, astute, and a legal whiz, Taylor was also Court's friend. He wanted what was best for her. He was also frighteningly forthright in his opinions. If Taylor had suspected for a moment that it wasn't in Court's best interests for them to get back together, he wouldn't have hesitated to tell Nick precisely that.

Taylor's assurance did a great deal to allay Nick's second thoughts and fears. The thought renewed his self-confidence. It fired his convictions. It gave him the ambition to start on the bathroom.

By the time Julie and Taylor convinced Courtney that it was time to call it a night, she was considerably calmer than she had been when she arrived at their apartment. She was also resigned to the inevitability that she was going to have to live with Nick until the baby was born.

That didn't mean she liked it any better than she had, but she accepted it.

For now, anyway.

Sounds of traffic washed over her and reflections of lights on the street below floated across the ceiling as Courtney listened and watched from the bed in Julie and Taylor's guest room. In the city, it was never truly dark or silent, a fact that she had never noticed until that ski trip when she'd met Nick.

It had been different in the Poconos. It had been both dark and silent. Closing her eyes and covering her ears didn't quite simulate the way it had been there because the light and sound still filtered through her eyelids and fingers. On the still, moonless nights at the lodge, her room had been so pitch black that she couldn't see her hand in front of her face and so quiet that she could have heard a pin drop.

Her first few nights there had been a revelation. All the darkness and silence had kept her awake. It had been positively eerie, disorienting, as if she were in a void. To be perfectly honest, the sensation had been sort of frightening.

Until Nick.

When she had slept in Nick's arms, the darkness and silence had become something else altogether. Like a comforting blanket, it had enveloped them, shielding them from the rest of the world. At the same time, it had also been excitingly sensual and wildly erotic, heightening her senses so that every whisper and kiss and caress had seemed more intense than any she had ever known. . . .

Nick's fingers slipped across her bare midriff, lightly tracing her bottom rib as his knuckles grazed the rounded underside of her breast. Simultaneously, his warm, moist breath caressed the rim of her ear. Drifting somewhere between wakefulness and sleep, she responded to his touch, arching her back, curving her bottom into the cradle of his hips. Her low purr of arousal mingled with Nick's answering growl and the provocative chord echoed in the darkness of the room.

His lips nuzzled the soft skin behind her ear, nibbling delicately, teasingly. Shivering, she rolled her head against the pillow, exposing more of her throat to him. He took full advantage of her offering, exploring more and more of her throat with his mouth as his hand moved up to capture her breast. He cupped it, his thumb gliding over the nipple, coaxing it into a hard peak that ached for more of his touch. She pressed herself more firmly into his palm, at the same time molding her buttocks against his hardness . . .

With a swift, steadying intake of breath, Courtney hauled herself forcibly back into the present. She had to keep herself under control and forget about the past. There was no future for herself and Nick. There couldn't be, no matter what her body wanted. She told herself that she was grateful that Nick didn't want her as anything other than the mother of his child.

Across town, in Courtney's apartment, Nick lay awake and restless in her bed. Faced with the prospect of God only knew how many nights sleeping on the sofa, he'd decided to take advantage of the empty bed that had presented itself when she had stayed to spend the night with Julie and Taylor.

It had been a mistake of the greatest magnitude. The sheets, pillows, and blankets all smelled of Court. If he analyzed the scent, he could pick out each of the notes of its fragrance—the Opium and Obsession that she alternated between, the almondy Vidal Sassoon, and the heady scent that belonged only to Court. He couldn't stand it. Sleeping alone surrounded by that smell was a torture calculated to drive him right over the edge.

Groaning, he rolled over, trying to suppress the arousal that Court's scent had evoked. The only thing that accomplished was to bury his face in her pillow, heightening memories that were already too acute for him to bear. Unbidden, vividly erotic images crawled from the recesses of his mind to haunt him. Images composed entirely of smell and taste, created by the distinctive aura that could belong only to Court. Again, he was confronted with the memory of how she'd tasted when he'd explored every inch of her with his mouth. . . .

His tongue dipped into the hollow behind Court's ear, capturing the sweet tang of her skin and testing it against his memory. Every time it had the same effect on him, as if he were tasting it for the first time. It was subtle and tantalizing, enticing him to taste it again and again, arousing him beyond anything he had ever known.

Slipping over her jaw, he brought his mouth to hers, sipping at her, absorbing the tastes of margaritas and cinnamony toothpaste and a more potent variety of the aphrodisiac that was implanted in her skin. Seeking more, he explored her depths, and his senses went wild.

He knew that Courtney was as aroused as he was. It wasn't the soft whimpers that escaped her lips, or the hands that reached for him, or even the small tremors that shook her body. It was the hot, sweet smell of her desire that assaulted his senses in a fundamentally primitive manner. Eradicating thousands of years of civilization, it provoked instincts he had thought were long since evolved out of the species, the need to mate, to possess in the most fundamentally basic way. Slowly, his lips moved downward across her body, following a primal path toward its source, the core of her femininity. . . .

Nick shot upright in the bed, gasping for air, trembling as he buried his face in his hands. He couldn't let himself think like this. If he did, he'd never be able to keep up the pretense that the baby was what mattered while he tried to win back Court. Allowing his desire to show through now would only send her running again. At the same time that he reminded himself that it was necessary to his plan, he didn't have the slightest idea how he was going to do it without going out of his mind.

When Courtney came into her apartment the following morning, the first thought to enter her mind was that she had somehow let herself into the wrong apartment. There weren't any shoes in the front hall. She had an overwhelming urge to turn around and check the number on the door immediately. She was finally reassured that this was really her apartment by the formidable presence of Nick on her sofa, a mug of coffee cradled in his hands, his feet resting on the smooth, bare surface of the cocktail table as he watched the *Today* show.

He turned his head and smiled in greeting as nonchalantly as if she'd just gone out minutes earlier for a loaf of bread. "Morning, Court."

Courtney stared at him openmouthed, stunned by the change in the way the apartment looked. Either he had worked all night, hired maids at super-premium overtime rates, or there was one hell of a mess shoved in a closet somewhere. Regardless, she was speechless.

"Are you allowed to have coffee? Decaf?" He had vaguely recalled one of his sisters complaining about having to make the switch from regular coffee to decaffeinated during her pregnancy.

She nodded wordlessly. At the moment, she needed something stronger, but she couldn't, because of both the hour and the baby.

"Come on, then, sit down," Nick continued, rising from the sofa and offering her his seat with a gallant gesture. "I'll get it for you."

By the time he had returned from the kitchen, Courtney had recovered from her shock sufficiently to have moved to the sofa. She was staring in the general direction of the television, although not a word of Deborah Norville's interview with some up-and-coming starlet was registering. Numbly, she accepted the mug from him.

Nick settled on the sofa beside her, smiling to himself as he pretended not to notice the extent of her reaction. He felt like some sort of miracle worker, even though he knew that the transformation never could have taken place in such a short time if he hadn't been trying to work off extreme frustration. "I made lasagna. What time do you think you'll be home tonight?"

Courtney blinked several times as she became aware that he had asked her a question that required an answer. She couldn't have said what the question was, and she certainly didn't have an answer for it.

"Court? Are you in there?"

"Hmm?" She sipped at the coffee, hoping that something of what he'd said would come to the surface of her brain.

Nick chuckled in amusement. "I'd forgotten . . . You're never at your best in the morning, are you? I just asked what time you'd be home for dinner."

"I know," Courtney snapped. "I was just thinking."

He knew darn well she was lying through her teeth; she'd been so far out in the ozone that she'd hadn't had the slightest notion what she'd said. "Could you maybe speed it up a little? I have a lot to·do here today."

Like what? she asked herself. Regrout the bathroom tiles? Build furniture for the baby's room? Make water into wine? Aloud, she answered, "Six. I'm usually home by six."

"You want to eat about seven, then?"

"Sure . . . No, I can't," Courtney contradicted herself. "Today's Thursday, isn't it?"

Nick nodded.

"I have Lamaze class on Thursday."

"What time do we have to be there?" he asked levelly.

"We?" Was he really back to this again? "Julie's going with me."

"Not any more."

FIVE

If Courtney hadn't been so addled that morning, she would have remembered how much touching natural childbirth entailed and she never, ever, under any circumstances, would have agreed to allow Nick to replace Julie as her partner. It was bad enough having him living in her apartment, but taking the class with him was an exercise in self-torture.

The instructor kept reminding her to relax, but Courtney was certain that it was a physical impossibility. How could she relax when she was lying flat on her back, her knees raised, and Nick seated Indian-style on the floor beside her? The hard thigh brushing her hip and the big hand resting on the curve of her abdomen sent her blood pressure right through the ceiling. Nick touched her and her senses ran riot; it was as simple as that. His ability to treat her with the same impersonal consideration that he would direct to any pregnant stranger didn't negate her reaction in the least.

She wasn't sure which made her angrier, Nick's ability to distance himself from any recognition of a relationship between the two of them that would have resulted in her condition or her own reaction to him. Either way, she wanted to flay him as a matter of principle. She gritted her teeth and tried not to let it show.

The other women in the class were all there with their husbands or lovers, a fact that she had noticed the first time she came with Julie and then promptly disregarded. It was brought back to the surface of her consciousness, painfully, by the couple next to them.

They were very young, about ten years younger than she and Nick, married less than a year, and effusively enthusiastic about the baby, their new marriage, and each other. They were positively adorable together and, at the moment, it was more than Courtney could stand. They touched each other constantly, warmly, lovingly, sharing the experience of pregnancy. Each time they finished one of the exercises, they kissed.

Courtney clenched her teeth, wishing the couple had chosen a Lamaze class in New Jersey or Connecticut. In an effort to ignore them, she forced herself to concentrate on how angry she was with Nick. Mentally, she plotted the perfect murder.

Court had passed merely furious a good hour ago and gone straight to livid. Her violet eyes told Nick in no uncertain terms that she was less concerned with birth than with death. His death. And he had a sneaking suspicion that she wanted to torture him first.

Not that she needed to devise a torture for him. She couldn't possibly invent one more effective than this self-inflicted exercise in masochism. Everything about natural childbirth was so . . . intimate. It all reminded Nick of how they had gotten there in the first place. Nobody had warned him that there was so much touching. And just touching Courtney made him want so much more that it took every ounce of willpower he possessed not to sweep her into his arms and carry her home to bed. A shared bed. If she'd given him the slightest indication that the feeling was mutual, he would have pitched willpower right out the window.

She didn't, of course. As far as Nick could tell, the only effect his touch had on her was to make her even angrier than she already was, a feat he hadn't considered possible. He hadn't expected an instant or easy capitulation and it was only the second day of his campaign, but he had at least hoped to see some sign that he was doing the right thing. A smile, a civil word, anything except this steadily increasing hostility.

He couldn't take his eyes off Court, either, because he couldn't bear to look at the other couples in the room. They were all so much in love, so secure in their relationships that he was overcome by the most intense surges of insane jealousy toward them.

Especially that couple next to them. Even now, they couldn't keep their hands off each other. It was an agony to watch them, always touching and kissing. They laughed together as they felt the baby move within her and Nick was filled with renewed envy.

In an effort to quell the emotion, he concentrated on the breathing exercises, his hand on the curve of Court's belly. When he felt another of the subtle flurries against his palm, the pain tore through his gut again and he looked directly into Court's violet eyes, silently asking her whether it was the baby moving or her stomach growling. When she didn't answer, it hurt too much to have to voice the question aloud.

Two weeks later, Nick walked into a small Italian restaurant on the East Side, chosen specifically for its location. No one from Wall Street ever ventured this far north for lunch, making it improbable that Court would see him there with Steve. It was also late for lunch, almost two o'clock, so the dining room was almost empty and Steve was the only person seated at the bar. He grinned in wry amusement when he saw Nick.

"Hey, buddy, all this cloak-and-dagger stuff is ridiculous. You know that, don't you?"

Nick nodded, admitting the humor of the situation. "Don't take this the wrong way, pal, but I feel like I'm having an affair behind Court's back."

"I think it's all this skulking and secret arrangements." Steve peered at his best friend with open concern. "Nicky, are you aware that you look like hell?"

Nick winced and nodded. "I feel worse."

"Things aren't going well?"

"*That* is the understatement of the year." He was no closer to reconciling with Courtney than he had been when he had moved in with her. He was also exhausted from lack of sleep, had dishpan hands, and was suffering from terminal, unrelieved arousal. "She hates me, Steve."

"I told you she would."

"Thanks for the confidence. Remind me to give you a call when I'm really feeling low, so you can kick me."

"Let's get a table and talk. I need food."

"Long night?"

Steve nodded and grinned, wiggling his eyebrows mischievously. "Redhead. Natural."

Nick shook his head and looked around for the hostess. "Steve, why don't you find some nice girl and settle down?"

"Me? No way. It's too much trouble. Look at you."

"Court and I are hardly typical."

The hostess raced over to the pair at the bar, a stack of menus tucked under her arm. Together, Nick and Steve never had to make any sort of effort to be noticed. They stood out in any room, no matter how crowded. Only part of it was their size; in addition, they might have been designed to serve as perfect foils for each other. Steve's blond, blue-eyed, bronzed good looks were the ideal contrast for Nick's darkness, a combination that had been largely responsible for their success in the world of professional tag-team wrestling. At the moment, neither of them was cognizant of the spectacle they made by the mere act of crossing the room.

They settled at the table. Steve glanced over the menu briefly and then leaned across toward Nick, lowering his voice as he spoke. He couldn't have asked the question of anyone else, nor could anyone else have asked it of Nick. "If it's none of my business, tell me, but I have to ask. You and Court aren't dumb kids. How'd the two of you let her get pregnant?" As roommates on and off since before the time that they had gotten matching tattoos of their fraternity crest, they had shared so much of their lives that almost nothing was forbidden territory.

Nick didn't take offense at the bluntness of the question because he understood that it was an honest question, asked out of concern rather than voyeuristic curiosity. Leaning forward, he spoke quietly. "The specifics of it are none of your business, but you, of all people, ought to be told that birth control isn't infallible."

Steve slumped back in the chair, turned white under the tan, and choked, "It's not?"

"No." Nick picked up the menu and studied it before throwing out, "And the law of averages is going to catch up with you one of these days. I'm just very lucky that it happened with Court."

Steve considered the thought, gulped, and shifted uncomfortably in his chair. Disturbed by it, he changed the subject. "So what do you do with yourself all day? Watch soap operas?"

"Keeping up with that mess that Court calls an apartment is a full-time job. It's no wonder her housekeepers all quit." There were times when he suspected that Court was going out of her way to make the job more difficult than it already was.

"There's a concept. The Brawny Buccaneer, a house-husband."

They were interrupted by the arrival of the waiter to take their orders. After he left, Nick said proudly, "I'm learning how to cook.'' He'd been in constant telephone contact with his sisters, whom he called frequently for assistance. Although he alternated between them, he knew it was just a matter of time before they compared notes and began to wonder about his sudden interest in domesticity.

''Why don't you just go out to eat?''

Nick shook his head adamantly. ''Court hasn't been eating right. The only way I can make sure she does is to feed her at home.''

Abruptly, Steve changed the subject. ''Nick, Mike's doctor says he can start to work out next week, and he and Greg'll be going out on tour together.''

''Do you have a copy of our schedule?''

Puzzled, Steve nodded, extracted it from the inside pocket of his blazer, and handed it over. ''Why?''

Nick fixed him with a look of genuine bewilderment. ''Figuring out which dates I'll be able to make. Now on this Baltimore–Washington run . . . I can make one or the other, but both of them would have me out of town for five days . . .''

''Nick, what do you want me to do? I can't just sit around and twiddle my thumbs while you play house.''

''Playing house? Is that what you think this is? Some kind of game?'' Nick snarled, angry at the question in a way he'd never been angry about anything that Steve had asked before.

''Sorry, Nick,'' Steve muttered self-consciously, wondering if he should have said something to Nick before Jake started looking for a new partner for him.

''You damn well better be,'' Nick continued, leaning forward, his fists clenched on the tabletop. ''Right now, Court and the baby are the most important things in my life. We've been friends a long time, but if you can't understand that . . .''

The waiter arrived with their veal and Nick didn't get to finish his threat. It was probably just as well, because he had very nearly flushed fifteen years of friendship down the drain. By the time the waiter left, the tension that had risen between them had been broken.

"Look, Steve, if it's the money you'd lose not working," Nick began in an effort at making amends, "we can work out something. I can't afford to make it all up to you, but . . ."

"Nick, it's not the money . . ."

"Or maybe Jake could set up a few one-on-one matches for you . . ."

"To be honest with you, Jake's already talked to me about it . . ."

"And?"

"And . . ." Steve took a deep breath and exhaled slowly before he confessed, ". . . Jake's talked about looking for a new partner for me."

Stunned into silence, Nick stared at Steve.

"Nicky, I told him not to do anything until I talked to you."

"We have a contract . . ."

"Which you broke two weeks ago."

"I had to come back to New York!" Nick protested.

"I know that. But the fact of the matter is, you are not operating from a point of strength right now. If Jake doesn't want to renegotiate your contract, legally, he doesn't have to."

"Damn it, Steve . . . what can I do?"

"For starters, you can show up this weekend at the Garden . . ."

"I fully intend to be there."

"And beyond that?"

Nick sighed deeply, his head dropping back as he covered his eyes with one huge hand and admitted, "Beyond that, I just don't know. . . ."

Courtney leaned forward, her elbows propped on her desk as she shuffled through the pile of papers yet another time. She couldn't find the file for that stupid insider information business, and Peter McGuinn had asked to see it before the end of the day. It irked her that he didn't trust her enough to let her handle it herself, although she knew that more important things rested on the case than one of her clients and her relationship with him; the whole reputation of the firm was at stake.

Suddenly, it occurred to her that Maggie might know where it was, and she reached across the desk for the intercom switch. Before her hand got there, however, it buzzed, and she pressed down the button to speak. "Yes, Maggie?"

"Ms. Welsch, Julie Killian's here to see you," Maggie's voice carried through the intercom.

"You haven't seen the Striker file anywhere, have you?"

"I Xeroxed a copy for Mr. McGuinn and refiled it. Would you like to see it?"

"Thanks, Maggie. No, I don't need it. I was just . . . Send Julie in, would you?"

Courtney shook her head and sighed. She was lucky that Maggie was on top of things, because *she* certainly wasn't. Ever since Nick had moved in with her, she'd felt like something out of the *Night of the Living Dead*. If she were any more distracted, she'd be dangerous:

"So, how's that gorgeous hunk?" Julie asked without preface as she swept into the office, more chipper than usual. The last of the eternal optimists, nothing seemed to bother her. But then, it wasn't her life that was in a shambles, so she didn't have to worry. "You aren't still making him sleep on the sofa, are you?"

Courtney's look of utter exasperation answered the question.

"Court, really . . . Are you out of your mind?"

Courtney had asked herself the same question several times in the last two weeks, although for entirely different reasons. "Apparently. I let him move in, didn't I?"

"Come on now, Court, you might be able to fool some

people with that line, but I'm not one of them. I've known you too long for that." In spite of the virulent way Julie criticized Nick to his face, she made no secret of her opinion that she thought Courtney ought to give him another chance.

"I've also known you too long to accept any of your advice without a long, hard look at it." It was a lie and they both knew it. Courtney had never been able to stand up to Julie for a moment.

"Don't be ridiculous, Court. You still love Nick and you're just making both of you miserable by denying it."

She wouldn't admit it, but it was true. The last two weeks had made that fact abundantly clear to her. Although Nick hadn't shown the slightest interest in her except as the mother of his baby, it had been all she could do to keep from throwing herself at his feet.

"You look like you haven't had a decent night's sleep in days," Julie continued mercifully.

It was an astute observation. Courtney couldn't concentrate, she couldn't sleep, and it was starting to catch up with her. Three more months of this was going to make her a basket case. In spite of that, she retaliated sharply, "Anything else, Julie? Did you wake up this morning and say, 'Today, I'm going to go insult Court until I make her crazy'?"

"Of course not!"

"It sure seems like it, kiddo." Julie knew precisely where all her vulnerable points were, and she hit every one of them with unerring accuracy.

"I came to take you to happy hour." Julie could act affronted better than anyone else that Courtney knew. It always made her feel guilty; it was supposed to.

She wasn't going to let it bother her this time, she told herself. She was going to fight it with logic. "Julie, I'm not allowed to drink. You know that."

"Ginger ale."

"All that sugar . . ."

"Diet Coke."

"Caffeine and sodium . . ."

"For God's sake, then, a crummy glass of grapefruit juice."

Julie was certainly determined this time. It made Courtney wonder what she was up to. Whatever it was, she couldn't resist baiting her. "It gives me gas."

Julie rolled her eyes heavenward. "Did it ever occur to you that I just want your company? We haven't seen each other for two weeks, and you were all upset then."

"I'm still upset. Julie, a man I thought I knew that it turns out I really didn't know at all has moved into my apartment and taken over my life. He cooks, he cleans, he does my laundry . . ." He had her at the brink of insanity.

"And you're upset? If Taylor did half of what Nick does . . ."

"It would make you every bit as crazy as I am. How would you like living with someone who keeps force feeding you vitamins? I don't have any privacy anymore, Julie."

"So, come out with me, Court. Just us girls. We'll sit around and have a chat like old times. How long has it been since we've done that?"

Courtney grinned and conceded defeat. "Ages."

Julie returned the grin, knowing she had won. "See, you need some time out on the town. Anyway, Taylor's got some meeting tonight, so we can go out to dinner, maybe do some shopping . . ."

"I could use some hose . . . and more bras . . . mine are all getting too small again."

Julie looked at Courtney's chest and then down at her own meaningfully. "You see, there are a few advantages to this pregnancy thing . . ."

Towed along in Julie's wake, Courtney considered that a bigger bustline did not compensate for the other effects that pregnancy was having on her body. She could feel her feet and legs swelling, and she grabbed Julie, bringing her to a halt in front of the hosiery counter in Bloomingdale's.

"What are you looking for?" Julie asked.

"Support hose."

Slipping her hand inside the sample, Julie eyed it suspiciously. "They look orthopedic."

"They are orthopedic." Purposefully, she selected a half-dozen pairs in her size.

"But, Court . . ."

"Before you make one single objection, look down at my ankles.

Julie did. "Oh."

She didn't say another word as Courtney went to the counter with them, digging her charge plate out of her purse.

In the lingerie and foundations department, Courtney headed straight for the sensible bras, in spite of Julie's efforts to sidetrack her. "Look at this, Court," she said, holding up a silky blue negligee that she had picked up on their sweep through the department. "The color's perfect for you, and there's some fullness below this raised waistline . . ."

"Put it back, Julie," Courtney told her, selecting several possibilities and moving toward the fitting room. "I'm here for bras."

"That doesn't mean you can't look at anything else."

"If you like the nightgown, Julie, buy it. You don't need my approval. I'm sure Taylor'll love it."

"It's not my color at all, Court. It's you . . ."

Courtney sighed wearily.

"I bet Nick would like it."

Closing her eyes, Courtney leaned against the wall. Sure Nick would like it . . . if he had any interest in her. She shook her head and blinked fiercely, fighting back a wave of despair. Not for the first time, she reminded herself that it was simply the result of hormones gone haywire, the perfectly natural ups and downs of pregnancy.

"Are you okay, Court?" Julie asked with sincere sympathy.

Courtney took a deep breath and convinced herself that she didn't want to cry . . . not right in the middle of Bloomie's lingerie department. "I'm just a little dizzy," she lied.

Hanging the negligee on the nearest rack, Julie patted Courtney's arm consolingly. "You just go try on your bras and we'll get out of here . . . go get something to eat."

"Where the hell have you been?" Nick roared angrily.

When Courtney had unlocked the door to the apartment, the doorknob had been snatched out of her hand before she could turn it. He reached out, grabbed her by the wrist and dragged her into the front hall, slamming the door behind her.

Shocked by the ferocity in his eyes, Courtney stared up at Nick speechlessly. He loomed over her like a great avenging giant.

"Well, Court?" he demanded.

She still couldn't come up with an answer. She felt tiny and vulnerable and helpless against his fury.

"Why didn't you call?" Nick continued to rage. "What about dinner? What about Lamaze class?"

"That was tonight?" Courtney asked weakly.

"It's Thursday, isn't it?"

Courtney nodded, after she thought about it for a moment. She's been so confused, she didn't know what day it was anymore.

"And class is on Thursday, isn't it?"

She nodded again.

"So where were you?"

"Shopping . . . with Julie," Court stammered. As proof of her claim, she held up the bags.

Nick took a deep breath and let it out slowly, getting a grip on himself. He was so relieved to see her that he wanted to throw his arms around her. He'd been so frightened when she hadn't shown up for dinner, a condition intensified when he hadn't heard anything from her by the time they would have left for class. "Why didn't you call, Court?"

She caught a hint of something in his voice as he asked the question. If she didn't know better, she might have mistaken it as relief. She shrugged, ignoring it. "I didn't think of it, Nick. Julie showed up at the office and asked me to go, so I went."

"And it never occurred to you to call?"

"No."

The simple one-word answer scraped across Nick's nerves like nails on a chalk board. Gripping his fists so that his hands would stop shaking, he sputtered out, "Don't you think Julie would have called Taylor if you had shown up at her office and wanted to go shopping?"

Courtney stared at him incredulously. "That's completely different! Julie and Taylor are married!"

"You want to marry me, Court?" Nick screamed at the top of his lungs. "Is that what it will take for you to tell me something as simple as where you're going?"

All the color rushed from Courtney's face as Nick stormed at her. She'd never seen him like this before. It was such an appalling change from the sweet proposals that had haunted her for the last three months.

"Is that what you want?" Nick demanded, still shouting.

"God, no!" Court screamed back at him. Darting around him, she ran to the bedroom and slammed the door behind her.

The sound of the door kept her from hearing Nick's fist slam into, and through, the drywall.

Courtney kept her face buried in the pillow, hoping that its softness would muffle her sobs. More than anything she didn't want Nick to know that she was crying. He'd demand some sort of explanation, she was sure, and she wasn't prepared to give him one. Actually, she wasn't certain she could explain it to herself.

There were so many reasons she was crying that she couldn't have picked just one.

The situation between herself and Nick was hopeless. She couldn't have a professional wrestler in her life, not if she expected to maintain any sort of credibility at the firm. The partners would hate it, her clients would hate it, and, before long, she'd be the laughingstock of Wall Street.

And, although she wouldn't have admitted it for anything, she still loved Nick with everything in her soul. Keeping it a secret was killing her, but she had to do it. And even if she could have claimed Nick publicly as the man she loved, it was apparent that he didn't want her anymore. He was only there because of the baby. After the baby was born, Nick would be going, making intermittent appearances in her life to claim his rights as a father. If she let him know that she still loved him, he'd be able to tear her heart open again and again every time she saw him.

Nick could hear Courtney crying from the sofa. The bed he had hoped was only temporary was starting to look more and more permanent every day. He had to force himself not to go to her. He wanted to hold her, comfort her, tell her he hadn't meant anything that he'd said, but he couldn't do that. Before he moved in with Court, he had promised himself that he would wait for her to come to him. The way things were going, that seemed unlikely ever to happen.

Every one of her sobs tore through him like a knife, and he hated himself for blowing up at her like that. He hadn't meant to do it, but she'd scared the hell out of him with her little disappearance. Every possibility—from her being hurt to her running away from him—had occurred to him during the hours that he didn't know where to start looking for her.

Again, he reminded himself that his purpose in moving in with Court was to convince her that he still loved her and they belonged together; so far, all he'd accomplished was to hurt her more than he had before. The whole situation was a real mess, and more difficult than he'd anticipated. He had to rethink this and start over.

Long after Court stopped crying, he lay awake, considering his options.

SIX

This wasn't working out quite as well as Nick had hoped. In theory, living with Courtney gave them time to be together; in reality, he had to compete with her work for equal time. Weekdays, she always left for the office before seven-thirty and was never home before six. This hadn't particularly surprised him because he had known that her job was very demanding, particularly for a person driven to excel the way Court was. What he hadn't anticipated, however, was that Court considered weekends a time for her to complete all the research that she couldn't get done during the week. Her weekends began with *Wall Street Week* and ended with the Sunday *Times*. In between, there were the journals and information service reports. And the magazines.

The magazines were everywhere. Sometimes it seemed as if Courtney were doing her best to eradicate the entire tree population of North America single-handedly. Not only did she read all the usual business publications and all three major news weeklies, but there were fashion, entertainment, science, and art magazines, and a few more that he wasn't quite sure what their subject was. What any of them had to do with investments, he didn't understand.

Not that it really mattered. The point was that they occupied entirely too much of Court's time, as far as Nick was concerned. How was he supposed to conduct a campaign to win her back when he couldn't distract her from her work long enough to get her attention?

In an effort to regain the ground he'd lost the night before with his little tirade, he prepared Court's favorite meal, Beef Stroganoff. He set the table with her best china, silver, and linens. He added candles and flowers. Bringing out the heavy ammunition, he put Johnny Mathis on the stereo.

The minute that Courtney walked in the door, Nick knew that he had his work cut out for him. This was going to be even more difficult than he had anticipated. Her speculation and insider information case was going to the grand jury. She had been subpoenaed. The heat and humidity had rendered her feet so swollen that bedroom slippers barely fit. The baby was in training for the Olympic soccer team. And she had a large hole in the wall of the front hall.

She ate his lovingly-prepared dinner with nearly obscene haste and answered his repeated attempts at conversation with single-word responses. After she was finished, she fled for the living room, flipping off the stereo and replacing it with public television's salute to the finance community.

Forcibly concealing his discouragement, Nick followed her to the sofa, sat next to her, tucked an enormous shopping bag between his feet, and began to empty its contents onto the coffee table. The silent performance was calculated for the specific purpose of attracting Courtney's attention.

It worked. "What in the name of God is that?" She stared at what appeared to be an overgrown set of headphones for a portable radio.

"I've been reading about pre-natal education . . ."

"Excuse me?"

"Pre-natal education," he repeated levelly. "It sounds like a valid concept. They figure that the baby retains a lot of the knowledge even after he's born, allowing him to learn better as he . . . ."

"Get serious, Nick."

"I am." He reached into the bag, pulled out a tape player, and set it on the coffee table next to the headphones. "It's like a Walkman for the baby."

"I am not putting that thing on my stomach."

"Yes, you are." He dug a handful of tapes out of the bag. "Just think how good it will be for him. Math, science, history . . ."

"Forget it, Nick."

"Literature, art, music, languages . . ." Another handful of tapes accompanied his words.

"You've wasted your money, Nick, because I . . ."

"No, I haven't. Lie down, Court." He grasped her shoulders and turned her body, gently forcing her to recline against the cushioned arm of the sofa.

"Nick . . ." she protested through gritted teeth, struggling to sit up.

"C'mon, be a sport," he said, holding her there. He had his size and her altered center of gravity on his side.

"I don't want . . ."

"If you'll give it a try, I'll massage your feet and calves."

It was out-and-out bribery and they both knew it. Between the swelling and the cramping of her feet and calves, Courtney would have made a pact with the devil for relief.

She sighed wearily. "Okay, I'll do it."

Nick grinned in response, eased her back against the cushions, put her feet on his lap, and reached for the hem of her shirt.

"What are you doing?" she squawked, grabbing the hem out of his hands and yanking it back down over the waist of her shorts.

"I have to put the transmitters on your stomach," he answered with feigned innocence, tugging upward on her top.

Courtney eyed him suspiciously, retaining her grip on the bottom of her shirt. The last thing in this world she wanted was Nick adjusting her clothing in any way. It brought back too many memories that conflicted with her vow not to succumb to him.

"Court, it's for the good of the baby."

She continued to glare at him, not convinced.

"And you want a foot massage, don't you?"

Back to her aching feet again, her point of greatest vulnerability. She relinquished her grip on the material, dropping her hands to her sides.

Nick nodded with satisfaction and lifted her hem. It was his first glimpse of her bare belly since it had begun to expand with her pregnancy. It took every ounce of will-power he possessed not to run his hands over it, caress it, press his face into it. With a deliberately impersonal touch that disguised his emotion, he arranged the transmitters as the directions indicated, popped a cassette into the tape player, and started it before leaning back on the couch and taking one of her feet into his hands.

"All you have to do now is relax."

Courtney gave him a baleful look and turned her attention back to the television. She attempted to, anyway. She couldn't possibly concentrate with her shirt tucked up under her breasts, her stomach bare, and her foot in Nick's hands. Commodity futures took a distant second to Nick's calloused fingers kneading the aching muscles of her feet. It felt wonderful. She felt pampered and slightly decadent and couldn't resist responding to it. Her toes curled and her arch flexed against his hands.

He tapped her on the toes, scolding her. "I'm doing the work here. You're supposed to be relaxing."

She nodded meekly, too soothed to care that Nick was giving her orders and she was obeying them.

"C'mon, now. Close your eyes."

To his astonishment, she did.

Courtney allowed herself to drift, floating on the dual sensations of Nick's gentle touch and the soft droning of the tape recorder. She wasn't sure, but she thought he was teaching the baby Japanese. Slowly, he caressed her feet and legs, easing the painful cramps in her calves, soothing her puffy ankles and feet. Gradually the anxiety and resentment of the last week receded and were replaced by tranquility and drowsy contentment.

Nick wasn't certain precisely when Courtney dozed off, but he was pleased when he realized that she was asleep. It was a good omen, a sign that he was gaining her trust, and maybe some of her affection. It gave him renewed hope that he would be able to win her back. It also gave him his first real chance to look at her. Earlier, when she was still awake, he had forced his gaze away, but now he could indulge himself without her knowledge. Sure, it was voyeurism of the most flagrant kind, but if any man were ever entitled, it was he.

She was so beautiful, swollen with his child, more beautiful than he had imagined. Her thin frame was now rounded and her breasts were fuller, emphasizing her delicate femininity. One of his hands released her ankle of its own volition and stole upward to her abdomen, at first touching it gently and then stroking its taut surface.

It had never been his intention to awaken her. The way things were going, he didn't know when he'd get another opportunity to touch her again. It was too good to last, however, and he sensed when her eyes fluttered open, catching him in the act.

At first he felt a surge of disappointment, then embarrassment. He hesitated before he raised his eyes to hers, not wanting to see the hostility—or worse, contempt—that he fully expected to find there. Steeling himself, he finally forced his eyes to meet hers and he saw something there that he hadn't seen since before he left for Boston almost four months earlier. When he'd seen it then, he'd told himself it was love. He almost dared to believe that it might still be. He gazed into the glowing violet depths, torn between pursuing it and backing away, fearing what her reaction would be. For all he knew, she might clobber him with something really lethal this time.

With a sudden, distinct kick against his palm, the baby made the decision for Nick. He gasped, awestruck at his first definite contact with the baby, his eyes glided down to the skin beneath his hand, and he stared, mesmerized, at the spot until Courtney's small hand moved to cover his. Encouraged by the gesture, he raised his eyes to meet hers again. The look he had seen there before was even stronger. He dared to believe.

Nick reclined on the sofa, easing his long body between Courtney and the sofa's back. His hand still beneath hers, he brushed his lips softly across her temple and murmured, "Thank you."

With a swift intake of her breath, Courtney ordered herself not to respond to him. The choked quality of her answer testified to her failure. "For what?"

"The baby," he whispered. "Our baby, Court. You could have gotten rid of it, but you didn't. You were so mad at me . . ."

She closed her eyes in a futile attempt to block out the hypnotizing quality of his voice. The pressure forced out a single shimmering tear. "I couldn't, Nick. I wanted . . ." Her voice faltered. Her mouth was as dry as her eyes were moist, and she dragged her tongue over her lips.

"Why, Court? Why couldn't you?"

A teardrop on her other cheek mirrored the first as she shuddered and swallowed a sob. "I . . ."

Nick slipped one arm beneath her back and cradled her against his chest. "Shh, Court. Honey, don't cry. Please don't cry." He bowed his head to kiss away her tears.

The tenderness in his voice and his gesture made her cry even harder. "I couldn't . . . couldn't . . ."

"Shh, honey, you don't have to tell me. All that matters is that you didn't." His big hand caressed the narrow span of her back as his lips wandered over her face, exploring the familiar contours thoroughly before his mouth touched hers. His kiss was infinitely tender, demanding nothing, sweetly timid. Even after her lips parted in a content sigh, Nick reached down within himself, sought, and found a reserve of willpower that he hadn't known he possessed. Calling upon it, he willed his arms not to tighten around her. He willed himself not to moan with desire. He willed his tongue to remain in his own mouth. He told himself that, for the moment, the fact that she'd allowed his touch at all was enough and he shouldn't ask for more from her.

Courtney was overcome by the supreme delicacy of Nick's kiss. It reminded her all over again how surprised she had been the first time he had kissed her. He was so massive that she had never suspected that he could be so gentle and giving. She shivered as the memory mingled with the current reality, and snuggled into his arms, her hip tight against his loins. She began to return his kiss, and was frustrated when he didn't deepen it. She knew damn well that he was every bit as aroused as she was. In a desperate effort to provoke him, her tongue darted out to stroke the edge of his lip.

Nick groaned and shuddered, thrilled as he felt the dissolution of the barriers between them. He'd never dared to hope for such significant progress this quickly. His mouth opened against hers, demanding that she make the decision to go further.

Unable to resist, Courtney reached up, tunneled her fingers through his dark curls, and pulled his head down to hers. Her tongue plunged inside his waiting mouth, meeting his briefly before it withdrew.

He followed, desire rising in him.

The door buzzer from the lobby sounded, startling them both.

Nick swore vividly and buried his face in the sofa cushion. Courtney scrambled to an upright position and covered her mouth with one hand. He was pale. She was flushed. They both struggled to quell their arousal.

"Court, honey . . ."

"No, Nick, don't. That should never have happened." Her hands were clenched, white-knuckled in her lap. It looked like a distinct possibility that she was going to cry.

"Yes, it should have happened, Court. It's always been right between us. We're . . . Court, I . . ."

The buzzer sounded again.

Cursing again, Nick levered himself off the sofa and strode to the intercom. With barely-contained violence, he slapped down the "TALK" button and growled into it. "Yes?"

The doorman's voice filtered through, accompanied by noises that may or may not have been human. "Ms. Welsch?"

"Does this sound like her?" Nick snarled back.

"No, sir. There are some people down here that say they're here to visit her." He sounded skeptical.

"Do they have names?" Nick snapped back in exasperation.

"Hey, Nicky, it's me!" Although the speaker was nowhere near the intercom in the lobby, Nick recognized the voice at once.

"Send them up."

"Yes, sir."

Nick let go of the button, swore yet again, and returned to the living room. "Court, honey, Steve's here. I think he's got some other people with him."

"Steve?"

"My partner. You haven't met him yet. See, Court, tomorrow night there's a bout at the Garden."

She paled even more than he thought was possible. "Are you . . . ?"

"Yes." He sat down next to her, putting his arm around her waist.

She cringed. "Don't touch me!"

"Court, please . . ."

The pounding on the door, followed by a loud whoop, set Courtney's crying to even greater intensity. When Nick tried to comfort her, circling his arms around her and pulling her to his chest, she fought him. Although he held her firmly, he was careful not to hurt her. When the pounding continued, growing louder, he didn't know what to do. He couldn't just leave her there, sitting in the middle of the living room and crying, while he let in his friends. He couldn't let them continue their abuse on the door. Exasperated, he stood and swept Courtney into his arms.

"What the . . . ?" she protested.

"Honey, I'm just taking you into the bedroom so that I can let them in," he explained as he carried her across the room. "After you stop crying, you can wash your face and come out and meet them. You don't want them to see you this way, do you?"

"I don't want to see them at all!"

"Well, they're here," he said, laying her on the bed. "I'm sorry about their lousy timing. Come out later, please?" He leaned over her, pressing a swift kiss to her lips. "After they're gone, we'll talk."

Before she could protest, he turned and was gone.

Nick yanked open the door, revealing the crowd out in the hall. In addition to Steve, there was a decidedly unnatural redhead that was, apparently, his date; Khalid Abaza, known as "The Desert Fox," in spite of the fact that the only desert he'd ever seen was just outside Las Vegas; Khalid's wife, Selena, a tall, willowy ex-model; Marty "Bulldozer" Brennan; and Doug "The Highland Warrior'' MacLeish. Nick groaned inwardly. The last two did not inspire confidence for continued success in his reconciliation with Courtney. Socially unacceptable behavior was their trademark and, with them, it wasn't an act. Single-handedly, either of them could destroy all the headway he'd made with her; as a collective unit, they could undoubtedly get him pitched out the front door.

"Well, Nicky, aren't you going to invite us in?" Steve asked, flashing a smile that rivalled Nick's as he strode past his partner into the foyer, hauling the redhead with him. "Something happen to the wall?"

Nick's eyes rolled heavenward and then appealed to a more immediate source of help, Selena.

"Don't worry, Nick," she assured him. "They've all promised to be on their best behavior tonight."

"They've already failed," he muttered darkly.

"So where's your lady?" Doug thrust a pizza box at Nick and he grabbed it before it fell to the floor.

"Yeah. We all came to meet her." Marty followed Steve and Doug, lugging an ice chest. "Brought some beer."

Steve looked around and whistled softly. "Great place."

"Let's keep it that way."

Courtney lay on the bed, staring up at the ceiling and trying to empty her mind. She was afraid to think about what had happened with Nick and where it would have led if they hadn't been interrupted. He'd only been in her apartment for two weeks and already she was putty in his hands. At the rate she was going, by the time the baby was born, she'd have no defenses against him at all.

In an effort to bolster her resolve, Courtney reminded herself that there was no way on earth that she could possibly be in love with a man who appeared publicly clad in nothing but stretch pants, a mask, and a tattoo! She'd seen their women on television. They wore Lurex tube tops and leather pants and spike heels. It was too humiliating to consider that she could join their ranks, that she could have that horde in her living room on a regular basis. On a more practical and immediate note, she hated to think about what kind of destruction they were inflicting upon her living room at that very moment.

"Marty, put that back!" Selena snarled, not for the first time since they arrived at Courtney's apartment. "If you touch one more piece of her crystal, you aren't going to live to wrestle tomorrow night!"

"C'mon, Marty, you don't act like that when you come to our house," Khalid added. "Show Court the same consideration."

"Nick never cared how we acted when we visited him before," Marty complained.

Nick leaned forward, picking up Doug's glass from the coffee table and placing it on a coaster. "This isn't my place. It's Court's."

Selena recognized the subtle, despairing tone in Nick's voice. The poor man was so in love with Courtney, and he couldn't understand why she couldn't overcome his image. She and, to a certain extent, Khalid were the only ones in the room who could possibly understand how Courtney felt. During their courtship, the "Beauty and the Beast" jokes had sent her running from him on more than one occasion. Leaning across her husband, she touched Nick's arm to get his attention.

Nick looked over at Selena. His dark eyes confirmed what she had heard in his voice.

"Nick, let me go in and talk to her," she said quietly. "Maybe I can help."

He nodded gratefully before turning to rescue one of Courtney's Swavorski water lily candlesticks from Marty's clutches. The man was like a magpie; if it glittered, he couldn't resist it.

* * *

Courtney knew they hadn't left; she could still hear their voices, punctuated by an occasional loud laugh or shout, in the living room. No matter what Nick wanted, she wasn't emerging from her bedroom until they were gone. When she heard the door open and close again, she gritted her teeth, vowing that nothing he could say would change her mind.

"Go away, Nick," she muttered, her back remaining to the door.

"It's not Nick." The voice was husky and deep, but definitely female.

Courtney's head snapped around to confront the intruder.

"I'm Selena."

The introduction wasn't necessary; Selena's face had been featured on the cover of every fashion magazine in America since Courtney was seventeen. She was even more stunning in person, dressed entirely in the understated elegance of Calvin Klein. Courtney's eyes traveled up the long, thin legs that had been the bane of her existence ever since she had realized that she had reached her full height. Just before she'd learned that she was pregnant, Courtney had tried on the outfit that Selena wore and she had looked as if she were three feet tall.

"You must be Court. Nick's told me so much about you." Selena sat on the edge of the bed, pulling up her legs with the casual grace that was her stock in trade. Courtney tried not to think how ungraceful she was with her new bulkiness. "I think the two of us should talk."

Nick never knew what Selena said to Courtney, but the two women finally emerged from the bedroom. Courtney was pale but civil, even when Marty blurted out several unwelcome but predictable remarks regarding Italian virility and Doug elaborated on them. Steve looked uncomfortable at the immediate evidence of Nick's impending fatherhood, a reminder of their conversation the day before. His blood turned to ice when he noticed the blatantly envious looks that his date kept giving Courtney and he made a silent vow to himself that he was taking the woman straight home. Only Khalid seemed to be taking the whole thing in stride. Pulling out his wallet, he spent the next hour proudly displaying photographs of two-year-old Michael and bragging.

Nick was ecstatic that Courtney warmed to Khalid and Selena. He had feared that she wouldn't see any further than Marty and Doug and that . . . person that Steve had found Lord-only-knew-where.

Courtney liked Khalid and Selena. They negated everything she had believed about the world of professional wrestling and the people in it. They were normal, which was more than she could say for the woman with the pinkish-orange hair and pierced nose.

By the time they left, to both Nick and Courtney's astonishment, Courtney had agreed to accompany Selena to the matches the following night.

After the door shut behind their departing guests, Nick returned to the living room, where Courtney still sat on the sofa. Propping his back against one arm of the sofa, he reached to encircle her with his arms, drew her between his upraised legs, leaning back against his chest, and pressed a soft kiss behind her ear. "Thanks, Court. You were a real trooper tonight. You didn't have to be that polite to Doug and Marty. Anyone else would have tossed them out the window. And agreeing to go with Selena tomorrow night . . ."

"I liked Khalid and Selena."

"I knew you would. I wanted you to meet them months ago because I thought it would help you see that professional wrestling isn't what you thought it was. Still think it is," he amended. "You can get a better sense of what it's really like tomorrow night. I hope you can learn to like Steve, too. He's basically harmless."

She gaped at him, wide-eyed. "Nick, harmless men

rarely frequent places where they meet women who look like Charlene.''

Nick thought about it for a moment and then laughed. "She is a real prize, isn't she? I wonder where he found her.''

"Don't ask me." Courtney joined him. "I'm still wondering whether she's even human.''

"It doesn't matter. I'd bet my last dollar that Steve won't be seeing Charlene anymore. He'll probably drop her at her front door tonight and run. She looked like you were giving her ideas," he stroked her stomach meaningfully, "and it scared the hell out of him.''

"He looked like he was giving serious consideration to the merits of celibacy.''

"Knowing Steve, it won't last for long. He's too interested in good times while he's on the road to let good intentions get in his way." Courtney stopped laughing and Nick kicked himself mentally. He'd just convicted himself by association and he wasn't even guilty. "Court . . .''

"Hmm?" She sounded like she might start crying again.

"I'm not saying I was a monk, but I was never into good times, not like Steve. And there hasn't been anyone else since January and the Poconos. Since you.''

Courtney bowed her head and sniffed.

His arms tightened around her. "Please believe me, Court.''

She nodded. "I do." Nick's long-distance courtship had been so ardent that he couldn't possibly have found the time or energy for any sort of relationship with anyone else.

"Court?''

"Hmm?''

"I didn't come back or move in with you because of the baby. I did it because I'm still in love with you. The baby was just an unexpected bonus.''

Courtney shuddered with emotion at the confession.

"No matter how many times you told me to give up and go away, I couldn't, because I never stopped loving you and I believed that you loved me."

She did love him; it was just that loving Nick demanded too much that she couldn't handle, not the least of which was suffering through the personal and professional ridicule that disclosure of their relationship or marriage would engender.

"Do you?"

She nodded jerkily, like a broken doll.

"Can I sleep with you tonight?"

SEVEN

He breathed the request so softly that she wasn't sure she'd heard him correctly. She turned to face him, her violet eyes huge in her pale face. "What?"

"Please, Court . . . just sleep," he whispered, verifying what she'd thought he said. "I just want to hold you again . . ."

Courtney was torn. At the same time that the idea of sleeping in the strong circle of Nick's arms was irresistible, she knew what he really wanted. As he'd told her time and time again, as all of the cards and flowers had insisted, loving her and marrying were irrevocably linked in Nick's mind.

He saw the anguished uncertainty on her face and hated himself for breaking his self-imposed promise not to push her. "I'm sorry, Court . . . I can't help myself. I can't stand sleeping on this sofa another night, knowing that you're just on the other side of the wall. I don't want walls between us anymore."

She took a swift, shuddering intake of breath at his words. Every night for the last week, she had agonized over mental images of Nick lying half- or fully-naked on her sofa.

"Please, Court . . ." he begged.

"Nick . . ." She buried her face in her hands, wishing her body could go to bed with Nick and leave her head out of it.

He misunderstood her reticence. "I promise I won't make love to you, Court, not tonight."

Courtney met his eyes for the first time since just after he had asked to sleep with her. "You won't?"

Nick shook his head slowly. "I just want to hold you tonight—so badly it hurts."

Her violet eyes shimmered with unshed tears. "You don't want to make love with me, Nick?" she asked disbelievingly.

He smiled and then bent his head to kiss her gently. "I want to make love with you when you're ready. I'm not stupid or masochistic, and I'd have to be one or the other not to make love with you just because you wouldn't marry me. As it is, we've denied ourselves for too long because of it."

Courtney considered this. It was a new attitude for Nick. She wanted to believe that he had given up on marriage, but she didn't dare.

"You're sure? No more pressure about marriage?"

"No more pressure, but that doesn't mean I'll stop asking. If you're ever ready to take that step, I'll still want to marry you."

"And if I'm not?"

He shrugged and smiled. "Then I'll still love you."

"You understand, then?"

"Not really, but I'll learn to live with it."

"And I'll have to learn to live with the wrestling?"

"That's what tomorrow night's all about. Maybe Selena can help you learn to live with it."

"Nick?"

"Hmm?"

"Would you make love with me?"

"Tonight?"

"Now."

"No."

"What?" Her voice rose incredulously and she stared at him.

"Not tonight, Court," he replied firmly. "I said that all we were going to do tonight was sleep and I meant it."

"But . . . why? Don't you want to make love to me?"

"Yes, Court, I do, very much. But I won't make love with you until after tomorrow night."

"Why? 'Women weaken legs'?" she asked, repeating the famous line from *Rocky*.

"No, Court. I don't want you to have any regrets about it after you see what I do for a living. If you still want to make love after tomorrow night, we will."

Julie was right; the blue nightgown was perfect for her eyes and the design flattered her new shape. While Julie hadn't been looking, Courtney had tried it on and bought it, not because she'd thought Nick would like it, but because it was the first thing she'd had on in weeks that made her feel attractive.

She slipped it over her head and stood admiring her reflection in the bathroom mirror, telling herself it didn't matter that Nick had decided they wouldn't make love that night. She wanted to wear it anyway for their first night sleeping together in more than five months. It was a celebration that deserved more than a cotton Lanz nightgown.

When she re-entered the bedroom, Nick was in bed, experimentally arranging and re-arranging the sheet with a nervous agitation that surpassed the first time that they had made love. She stood in the doorway watching him as he first pulled it up over his chest, then pushed it back down to drape around his waist again. He glared down at his tattoo; apparently, he feared that it would remind her of all the obstacles that stood between them. When he reached for the T-shirt tossed on the floor next to the bed, Courtney stopped him.

"Nick, you don't have to do that. I've already seen it and, even if I hadn't, I won't be able to see it in the dark."

He turned to greet her and the smile vanished as his mouth fell open. He stared at her intently, his eyes misted over, and he finally croaked, "Lord, you're beautiful, Court!"

She stood frozen in the doorway, chewing her lower lip nervously, her head bowed in contemplation of her rounded belly. Even with the blue nightgown, she had never felt less beautiful in her life.

"Come to bed, sweetheart," he whispered, his dark eyes still fixed on her.

Courtney raised her head and met his eyes. She smiled. Nick thought she looked like a Madonna. He told her so.

She moved to climb into the bed and Nick put his arms around her, holding her lightly but firmly, as if he feared she were the fragile porcelain object he had imagined her to be when they first met. He kissed her tenderly but passionately. When she tried to prolong the kiss, however, he disengaged her arms from around his neck and switched out the light. Turning her on her side, he cradled her against his body so that they could sleep spoon-fashion. He pressed another kiss to her bare shoulder and said, "Good night, sweetheart."

"Good night, Nick."

They lay silently in the dark, waiting in vain for sleep. Each was too aware of the other's familiar smell, too sensitized to the pressure of the other's body, too tensely wanting, to sleep. Courtney shifted restlessly in Nick's arms, one foot sliding up his calf.

"Nick?" she asked, the puzzlement apparent in her voice.

"Hmm?"

"What are you wearing?" All the times she had slept

with Nick before, he had always been nude. Instead of rough hair and skin, however, she felt cloth.

His answering chuckle was filled with self-amusement. "Jeans."

She didn't answer. Her silence spoke volumes.

"I told you I wasn't going to make love to you tonight. I meant it. I just needed . . . a little . . . deterrence."

She moved her buttocks experimentally against his fly.

"What are you doing?"

"You have to ask?"

He swatted her rear. "I told you, Court, not tonight."

She stopped moving. "Just checking. Good night, Nick."

"Night, Court."

Silence fell over them again.

"Court?"

"Hmm?"

"Marry me?"

She gave a little laugh. "No, Nick."

He tightened his arms around her. "Okay. Just checking."

Madison Square Garden, the venue of the wrestling matches, was already jammed with a sell-out crowd when Courtney and Selena arrived. As they wended their slow way through the throng, Courtney gaped around her, astounded not only by the number of people who would shell out more than twenty dollars apiece for the dubious privilege of viewing professional wrestling, but also by the variety of types of people.

The stretch Lurex-clad women and the beer-bellied men didn't surprise her. Those, she had expected to see. Truthfully, she had expected to see more of them. What surprised her were the punk-rocker teenagers, suburban housewives, celebrities, yuppie businessmen, and little old gray-haired ladies that made up the bulk of the crowd. Courtney was unable to resist making the observation that, for the first time in her life, she had concrete evidence that the "statistically-ideal demographic educational strata" to which Jones from Research constantly referred existed outside his imagination.

Courtney gaped as the hottest young actor in Hollywood, accompanied by a well-known European royal, was surrounded by photographers, reporters, and autograph seekers. In their aborted attempt to escape, the couple collided with a Cub Scout troop, whose small members were less impressed with their notoriety than they were with what they believed to be a blatant effort to break into the T-shirt line. Chaos reigned as they protested the intrusion, giving the pair a chance to escape their determined pursuers.

"Come on, Courtney!" Selena hissed, tugging on her elbow and dragging her through the mob that had stopped to view the altercation. "We've got to get out of here!"

Courtney squawked in protest, but she followed. She had little choice; Selena's fingers were gripped about her arm like a vise. She careened into a pair of cowboys, simultaneously hearing a cry behind her.

"Hey, there's Selena! Forget about the princess!"

"Who's that with her?"

Selena's muttered curse and increased pace were the little encouragement Courtney needed to hurry after her. Khalid's wife, a celebrity in her own right, had obviously had enough experience with the circus that recognition could bring to know precisely what she was doing.

"Follow them!"

"Over there by that pillar!"

They darted around three small boys wearing T-shirts with pictures of Nick and Steve on them.

"What's with Selena? She never ran from us before!"

"She ducked us sometimes, but she never ran!"

"Who's that with her?"

Selena swore again profoundly and came to a sudden halt next to a souvenir stand selling replicas of championship wrestling belts. "Court, trust me," she muttered between her teeth. "Don't worry. You won't need to say a thing." With that warning, she turned to confront the mob at their heels.

The photographers and reporters caught up with them rapidly once they had stopped.

"Hey, Selena, why'd you run?" a heavy, cigar-chewing man in a green polyester suit panted.

"You never have before!" accused one of the jean-clad photographers.

"I also never had my cousin Chrissie with me, Foster," Selena lied smoothly, addressing the photographer by name. "She's not used to all this."

"You a big wrestling fan, Chrissie?" the green suit asked.

Courtney stared at him, stunned, for a moment, until Selena answered for her. "Chrissie's never been to a wrestling match before. She's been visiting us for a few weeks, so we thought she might want to come and see what Khalid does for a living. And you folks aren't giving her the best impression of all this, you know. She's not exactly up for the hundred-yard dash at the moment." She put her arm around Courtney sympathetically, drawing attention to her pregnancy.

Satisfied that Chrissie was no one of any importance to them and they had nothing to gain by staying, the photographers and reporters dispersed, allowing Courtney and Selena to continue their progress toward their seats.

"Lord, I'm sorry about that, Court," Selena said, the green eyes that had appeared on a thousand magazine covers pleading for forgiveness.

"It's not your fault," Courtney assured her.

"But I should have known that coming in here with me would draw attention to you."

"That's why you stopped?" Suddenly, Courtney understood her reasoning.

Selena nodded. "Running was only making them more curious about you."

"Which was why you told them I was your cousin."

Selena nodded again. "I had no intention of telling them who you really are, and if I hadn't given them some explanation, they'd have moved heaven and earth to find out who you were."

With that, Selena herded Courtney along to their seats. "I gave you Michael's seat, you know. He loves to come, but I have to admit that I'm looking forward to sitting next to someone who doesn't stand on the chair and yell for Daddy."

"I think I can safely assure you that I won't." The last thing she intended to do was call attention to herself. "Selena, how do you stand it?"

"The press or the wrestling?"

"Either. Both."

"Modeling is a high-visibility profession. So is wrestling. When I modeled, I was always news. So was Khalid. Together, we were a magnet for photographers. The first time we went away together for the weekend, camping, they followed us clear to the Adirondacks and stayed at all the surrounding campsites."

Courtney closed her eyes and groaned in sympathetic horror.

"They spent the whole weekend bickering about who could get the best picture of us. Trying to win, one of them unzipped the tent and stuck his camera in."

"What'd you do?"

"I cried. Khalid made mincemeat out of a two-thousand-dollar camera and threatened to do the same with the photographer."

"How long was it that bad?"

Selena shrugged and sighed. "It comes and goes. After the camping weekend, they went away for a while, but once we got engaged, they were there all over again. I think there were three press people for every guest at our wedding. And while I was pregnant with Michael, they followed me everywhere. I think they were hoping for exclusive pictures of the birth.''

"Doesn't it bother you that Michael's going to grow up around wrestling? It's so . . ." she paused, mentally groping for the word.

"Undignified?" Selena supplied helpfully.

"I've called it a lot worse."

"So have I. In fact, I threatened not to marry Khalid because of it."

Courtney snapped her head up and her eyes met Selena's. "You did?"

Selena nodded and smiled serenely. "Yep."

"So what happened?"

"I changed my mind."

"And gave up your career?"

"Not because of the wrestling. I gave it up when I had Michael. First I was pregnant and there wasn't much of a market for pregnant models in my salary bracket. And afterward . . . Blondes get stretch marks like mad and I had a Caesarian. None of the clients were willing to use a model whose entire body had to be air-brushed."

"I'm sorry, Selena, I didn't realize . . ."

"I'm not. I made a lot of money modeling and I never really spent any of it. And wrestlers make good money. The top ones like Khalid and Nick do, anyway."

"I still can't believe they pay people real money to do this."

"They most certainly do. Professional wrestling is big business now."

Courtney never heard what Selena said next; the words were lost amid the ear-blasting rock music and thunderous roar of applause and cheering that accompanied the abrupt fall of darkness. Conceding defeat, Selena shrugged helplessly at her and turned her attention to the spotlight that had appeared at the far side of the arena, highlighting Khalid, clad in a burnoose and flanked by two women in harem costume.

Courtney gaped at Khalid in disbelief. This snarling, muscle-bound cartoon character couldn't possibly be the husband of the lovely woman seated beside her, the same proud and doting father who had sat on her sofa the night before, displaying photographs of his two-year-old son. Every possible explanation for the transformation that presented itself to Courtney smacked of a science-fiction plot: demonic or alien possession, brainwashing, cloning, or schizophrenia.

A single sideward glance at Selena banished such conjectures as utterly ridiculous fancies. The man in the spotlight was Khalid. The quietly possessive manner in which the other woman looked at him left no doubt that he was her husband, the father of her son, and the man she loved completely. Selena would never like the wrestling or be enthusiastic about it the way so many of the other wives and girlfriends were, but she wouldn't allow it to destroy her love for Khalid or her marriage.

Khalid climbed through the ropes and entered the ring, raising his arms with a triumphant cry. Opposite him was a monstrously fat man with a shaven head and a monocle, dressed as a caped parody of one of Kaiser Wilhelm's soldiers. With him was a woman who could have been Marlene Dietrich's twin. The two men faced off threateningly and then retreated to their corners, where, with the assistance of the women, they disrobed until both were clad only in regulation wrestling garb. The two men contrasted dramatically. Khalid, in snug black trunks, was the epitome of masculine fitness. While not as massive as Nick, Khalid possessed the same hard strength that had first attracted her to him. His opponent, however, was the embodiment of Courtney's worst suspicions about professional wrestling. He was positively repulsive. She was kindly but truthfully grateful that his belly, which was bigger than hers, was covered by the tank-style suit he wore. Even so, the amount of pasty, flabby flesh revealed was appalling. Ungraciously, she considered that, in trunks like Khalid's, the man would resemble nothing so much as an albino walrus. Possibly a manatee.

The pair faced off and began to grapple. Every doubt that Courtney had had about accompanying Selena was validated as the pseudo-Prussian lifted Khalid over his head, threw him to the mat, jumped on him, and then rose to his feet to deliver several near-enough-to-appear-real kicks to Khalid's head and midriff. Although Courtney knew that none of them actually met its apparent target, she flinched at each of the blows. She cringed as the man climbed to the top of the side ropes and flung himself at Khalid again. She covered her eyes as he twisted Khalid's leg backward, pinning it with his own.

Selena nudged Courtney's shoulder and she reluctantly removed her hands from her eyes. Looking down into the lighted ring again, she saw that Khalid now straddled the massive belly of the other man, pushing down on his shoulders. Even as the larger man struggled with him, Khalid pinned his back against the mat. The referee, down on his hands and knees beside the pair, slapped his palm once on the mat and declared Khalid's victory.

The audience went wild. Although the noise level had been impressive throughout the match, now it was deafening. Chanting began for "The Desert Fox."

Both men remained in character as Khalid accepted their accolades. The two harem dancers raced into the ring, returning Khalid's championship belt to the victor. He brandished it over his head and let out another yell, which was rapidly echoed throughout the arena. The vanquished lay on the mat, looking as if it were conceivable that they might have to bring in a crane and hoist him out. The Marlene Dietrich look-alike knelt beside him, simultaneously reviving him and shaking her fist at Khalid.

Courtney's distaste for professional wrestling did not abate during the next four matches. If anything, it grew even more profoundly intense. The arrogant preening before the matches was repulsive, the elaborate personae of the wrestlers overly affected, the half-clad women garishly tacky, the victory rituals childish.

After one of the wrestlers draped an immense snake across his opponent and attempted to wrap it around him, Courtney shuddered and turned to Selena. "I'm sorry, Selena. I have to leave."

Great concern showed in the other woman's face. "Do you feel okay? Are you having some sort of pain?"

"I feel fine, Selena," Courtney assured her. "I just . . . I can't see Nick like this." She tried to rise from her seat, but Selena gripped her forearm, holding her there.

"You can't, Court. . . . You promised Nick."

"I never said I'd stay all the way until the end."

"So we won't stay until the end. Nick and Steve are next. Please stay . . . we'll leave after they're done."

"Please, Selena . . ."

"I never thought you were a coward, Courtney," Selena accused.

"Of course, I'm a coward!" Courtney hissed. "If I weren't, I wouldn't care what anybody thinks about Nick and me. But I do care what people think. I can't just flush my career down the . . ."

She was interrupted by a sudden dousing of the lights. In the darkness, chanting for the Buccaneers began. The vibration of thousands of pairs of stomping feet shook the floor of the arena. At last, a spotlight pierced the darkness, illuminating two masked men in tight black pants, capes, and cutlasses, one dark, the other blond, both huge and muscular and bearing identical Jolly Roger tattoos on their chests. With fisted hands raised over their heads, both emitted the piercing whoop that was their trademark.

The sound was the stuff of Courtney's worst nightmares and she cringed in a desperate, embarrassed effort to become part of her seat. Although all logic and Selena both assured her that no one could possibly know who she was, weeks of fearing discovery of what she considered to be her shameful secret had conditioned her to caution where Nick was concerned.

Selena, knowing precisely how Courtney felt, squeezed her hand in reassurance and leaned over to shout in her ear. "I had the same look the first time!"

Courtney nodded to indicate that she had heard the words, but she never took her gaze off Nick. He looked like every female's fantasy pirate who stepped off the cover of a romance novel. It was easy to imagine that he could sweep some helpless woman off her feet, carry her off to a tropical island hideaway, and ravish her. Certainly, his effect on her had been that dramatic, although Nick hadn't had to exert nearly that much effort. Even now, when she was too embarrassed to claim him, Courtney had to clench her hands to her lap to quell the vividly tactile memory of the way his bare chest felt under her palms.

Her attention focussed on Nick, Courtney didn't take notice of the other pair of wrestlers until all four men were in the ring. When she did, she gasped with abject horror. They looked like a pair of escapees from the state hospital for the criminally insane, an impression confirmed by their appallingly sub-human behavior. By all indications, they would kill or maim for the sheer fun of it, like characters out of a low-budget, blood-and-guts thriller. The thought gave Courtney chills and she entertained the same ridiculous notion that always seized her when she watched such movies on television: she wanted to yell at Nick to get out of the house.

She repressed the urge. For the time being, anyway.

Courtney understood little about tag-team wrestling except for what Selena had told her in the cab on their way to the arena. Although there were two men on each team, only one of them was in the ring at any given time; the other waited his turn on the rim of the ring just outside the ropes. When the competing man tired or wanted out of the ring, he reached out to tag his partner, and the two men changed places. If either member of the team was pinned, that team lost.

Steve wrestled first for the Buccaneers. Courtney was grateful because there was always the possibility that the match would end before he tagged Nick. She didn't much like the idea of Nick setting foot in the ring with either one of those apparent psychopaths, a fear that was justified in the first thirty seconds of the match when Steve's opponent charged out of his corner like a crazed animal and hurled himself at Steve, knocking him face first unto the mat.

Steve didn't move. Although it alarmed Courtney, it didn't surprise her; the blow would have rendered King Kong unconscious. Courtney let out a small reflexive cry at the brutality of it and Selena offered her hand in comfort. Courtney gripped it gratefully and leaned forward in her seat, anxiously watching for any movement by Steve. He was so still. The homicidal maniac was so big and vicious, and he was still kicking Steve. She was absolutely terrified for him.

Steve's opponent grabbed his leg and twisted it, attempting to turn him over onto his back. At last, Steve took a deep, shuddering breath and stretched one arm up toward the ropes.

Simultaneously, Nick and the fourth wrestler rushed around the outside of the ring toward Steve. They got there at the same time and, as Nick reached out for Steve's hand, the other man pushed him. Nick teetered on the edge of the ring, threatening to fall.

Courtney's heart leapt into her throat.

Just as it seemed Nick's size was going to triumph over his coordination, he curled the fingers of one hand around the top rope, hauled himself back, and reached down to touch Steve's hand with his own.

"No, Nick!" Someone in the audience screamed shrilly. "Don't!"

Nick didn't heed the warning. The ogre torturing Steve

released him as Nick climbed into the ring. Snarling ferally, he pulled himself to his full height, which Courtney estimated at near seven feet, and turned his attention to Nick. The pair faced off as Steve crawled under the ropes to safety.

The vile creature lunged at Nick and Courtney heard a louder scream. ''C'mon, Nick, kill the bastard!''

Courtney's head snapped around, looking for the screamer. A full ten seconds passed before she realized that it was she. She, Courtney Welsch, respectable and normally dignified investments analyst, had become so caught up in professional wrestling that her body had risen to its feet and begun yelling of its own accord. Chagrined, she slunk back into her seat again.

Next to her, Selena was laughing. Not unkindly, but because she couldn't help herself. She wasn't sure which was funnier, the sight of Courtney screaming or the look on her face when she realized she was.

By the time Courtney recovered from her embarrassment, the match was over. Nick had pinned the escaped mass murderer to the mat. The spectators all cheered as Nick and Steve came to their feet, waved their fists over their heads, and whooped. Selena still couldn't stop laughing, even after she snagged Courtney's hand and hustled her from the arena.

_____ EIGHT _____

"Oh, Selena, I'm so embarrassed!" Courtney wailed. The two women had taken a cab back to Courtney's apartment, where they would meet Nick and Khalid. "Standing and yelling!" She cringed with humiliation at the memory. "How could I do something like that?"

Selena smiled gently, still amused by it. "If it makes you feel better, I'll let you chalk it up to hormonal rages. All pregnant women have them. Personally, I only cried a lot."

"About what?"

"Everything. Sad movies. The six o'clock news. Clogged drains."

Courtney nodded in sympathy. "Last week, I realized I was crying at Bugs Bunny cartoons."

"Switch to the Flintstones," Selena advised.

Both women laughed; just then, Nick and Khalid burst through the door, both of them also laughing.

"Hi, hon." Nick bent down, dropping a quick kiss on Courtney's lips. "So whadya think?"

Selena struggled to suppress a laugh and Nick and Khalid both looked at her seriously. "So what does that mean?" Nick asked.

Wide-eyed, Selena gazed at him innocently. "Nothing at all, Nick."

The two men exchanged glances that said they both knew the women were concealing something. Nick's eyes also told Khalid that, while he enjoyed his and Selena's company, he'd prefer to be alone with Courtney at the moment. Khalid's eyes answered that he understood completely.

"C'mon, Selena," he said, encircling her shoulders with one arm and propelling her to her feet. "We've got to get home before the sitter runs out of food and starts on the furniture."

"Hey!" she protested, moving forward toward the door. "That's my sister you're talking about!"

"I know. My sister's anorexic." He gave her another boost. "Bye, folks. If you get a chance, give us a call before we head out of town."

During their cab ride from Madison Square Garden to Courtney's apartment, Nick had threatened Khalid with dire, painful, permanently disabling consequences if he didn't retrieve his wife and get out as expeditiously as humanly possible. Khalid had taken the warning to heart, earning Nick's eternal gratitude and indebtedness.

"Court?" He crouched next to the sofa, his eyes on a level with hers. "Was it so awful? As bad as you thought?"

"Mm-hmm." She nodded, a sick look on her face as she considered what she had done. Jumping to her feet and screaming, indeed!

"Can you learn to live with it?" he asked anxiously.

She gulped. "Maybe," she answered uncertainly.

Nick brightened considerably. "Does that mean you'll marry me?"

Courtney closed her eyes and shook her head. "No," she breathed.

He cradled her chin in his big hand and she opened her

eyes. He looked into their purple depths hopefully. "Does it mean you'll make love with me?"

She smiled. Her eyes glowed. "Yes."

"With no regrets?" he checked.

"With no regrets," she assured him.

"Well, then . . ." With that, Nick scooped Courtney up into his arms and carried her into the bedroom. He placed her gently on the bed and stepped back to gaze silently down at her.

The black cloud of her hair beckoned him to bury his face in its silkiness. Her violet eyes, wide and bright, still possessed traces of the alluring innocence that had first attracted him to her. An innocence adamantly denied by the full red lips that knew precisely how to drive him mad. This time, anticipation was mingled with memory. And it had been so long.

Nick reached for the buttons on his shirt, fumbling clumsily as he tried to undo them. He hadn't had this much trouble undressing himself since he was two.

Courtney smiled patiently at the evidence of Nick's nervousness. He looked every bit as anxious as a man preparing to make love for the first time. He also looked every bit as sexy as she remembered. Maybe more so. His body was spectacular, hard and heavily-muscled and strong. What she could see of it. If only he could get his damned shirt off.

"Nick, come here," she breathed.

He stepped near the bed and she levered herself up to sit on its edge.

"Let me help you." She reached for him and began to unbutton the front of his shirt. As she undid each button, she leaned forward, pressing her lips against the newly-bared flesh of his chest.

"Oh, Court . . ." he groaned. "Do you have any idea what you're doing to me?"

"I bet I can guess." She cupped him with her hand through the denim of his jeans. "I was right."

He took a shuddering breath. "For God's sake, Court . . ."

Courtney smiled with feminine triumph and curled her fingers around him, stroking gently.

"Court!" His hand shot down to grasp her wrist.

"What's wrong, Nick?" she asked with seeming innocence.

"Court, darling, it's been so long . . . and I want so much . . ." Tears gleamed in his eyes. ". . . I'm afraid of hurting you. Or the baby. I've never made love to a pregnant woman before!" His voice rose at the last and his chest heaved as he gasped for air, struggling to regain control that was rapidly slipping.

She smiled in reassurance. "Yes, you have, Nick."

"Oh. You're right. You were pregnant before I left." He paused a moment, considering this. "But you weren't . . ." His hands moved descriptively. "Pregnant."

"You won't hurt me, Nick." Raising her arms, she slipped her hands inside his shirt and smoothed it from his shoulders, allowing it to fall behind him. She leaned close to him, flicking her tongue across his flat nipple. She blew lightly on the moist skin.

Eagerly, it responded, surging out from the wall of his chest toward her lips. Nick was trembling all over, his breathing was ragged and labored, and he wasn't sure, but he thought he was having a heart attack. A helpless whimper generated from deep within his throat, and he clenched his eyes closed.

Courtney showed no mercy. With more aggression than Nick had ever seen in her, she caught his erect nipple between her teeth and nibbled delicately. Her lips suckled it. Her tongue stroked it.

His knees collapsed and he dropped beside her on the bed, putting his arms around her to hold her tightly to him.

"No more, darling," he pled in a raspy whisper before taking her lips in a possessive kiss. "Please, don't torture me. I want you too much."

"I want you, too," she breathed against his lips. "Nick, please . . ."

Courtney peeled off her clothing, carelessly dropping each piece over the side of the bed to the floor as she removed it. At last, he saw her naked again.

In his mind's eye, Nick had pictured Courtney naked hundreds of times during the last five months. During the last two weeks, he had thought of little else. Now, in the flesh, she was different than he remembered. Jarringly different. Though the rational part of his mind had known that pregnancy would change her body, it still came as something of a shock to his system when he actually saw those changes. The glimpses he had had the night before had not prepared him for the sight of her, full and blossoming with their child. She was far more beautiful than he recalled. The natural wonder of conception and reproduction that had awed the ancients to honor femininity overwhelmed him and brought out a primordial part of him that he hadn't known still existed in modern man; he felt a surge of incredible wonderment. His hands cupped the mound of her belly and he pressed his face to it.

"Court, oh, Court . . ." he murmured against her. "I love you so much."

"Then show me." Her fingertips touched his cheek.

He turned his head to face her. There were tears of emotion streaming down his cheeks as he pressed a kiss into her palm. Turning her hand, she wiped them away with the backs of her knuckles. "Show me, Nick . . ."

Raw desire, fueled by Courtney's deliberate provocation, rose in him, blinding him to all else except the urge to claim her in the most fundamental manner, banishing control. He stripped off his jeans and covered her body with his, claiming her mouth. As his tongue searched its depths, his erection jutted against the juncture of her thighs, its hard and throbbing size graphically communicating his desire to her. Her legs parted instinctively and he knelt between them. His hands roved over her, gently yet arousingly skimming across her breasts, her stomach, and the dark triangle of hair that guarded the entrance to her womb.

He hesitated with that thought. Her womb. Their baby's shelter. Fresh tears rose in him.

"Nick?" Courtney asked, sensing the conflict in him, yet not understanding its cause. "What's wrong?"

Nick leaned over her, his weight on his elbows, and brushed his lips over her brow. "I want you so badly, I'm afraid . . . afraid I'll be too rough, too big. I don't want to hurt the baby, Court, or you . . ."

"You won't, Nick," she answered, her fingers digging into his hard buttocks, preventing him from rolling away from her.

Not reassured, he held himself back, trembling, his teeth clenched together as he loomed over her. Sweat beads stood out on his forehead from the strain. "I'm a . . ."

Courtney's hand slipped between them, grasping him, guiding him into her as she arched against him.

"Oh, Court . . ." he gasped. She felt so good, so right, surrounding him. Involuntarily, he moved within her.

Beneath him, she cried out, and he stopped, afraid. "Court?"

"Don't stop, Nick," she protested, hooking her legs around his thighs and moving against him. "It's wonderful," she urged him on in a hoarse whisper. "You're wonderful, darling! Please, Nick, love me!"

"I do," he groaned. Encouraged by her enthusiasm, the last of his fears put to flight, he kissed her ardently and rotated his hips in a demonstration of his desire. "So much, Court, so much . . ."

Together, they rose to the zenith, driven by the passionate kisses and tender caresses and exquisite friction of their lovemaking. With soft cries of triumph, they went over the edge, plummeting through space before they floated back to earth and reality, arms and legs twined around one another. Still linked intimately, they rolled to their sides, where they lay facing one another, stroking each other languorously.

Drowsily, Courtney smiled up at Nick, her head resting in the palm of his hand. "I love you, Nick," she whispered.

"Then why won't you marry me?" he asked quietly.

He felt her withdraw from him, as surely as if icy water had been thrown over them both.

"I can't," she choked, tears welling up in her eyes.

Miserably, he rolled to his back and stared up at the ceiling. "Oh, Court . . ." he groaned.

"Don't, Nick . . . Please don't ruin it."

"Don't ruin it, Court?" he demanded, his head pivoting to face her. Tears streamed downed his cheeks. "I love you. You love me. We're going to have a baby. How does wanting to marry you ruin anything?"

"I can't," she repeated. "You know that. You promised . . ."

"I promised not to pressure you. I didn't promise not to ask."

"Nick, don't . . ."

"No, Court!"

Putting his arms around her, Nick pulled her tightly to him. Courtney was stunned to feel his passion rising against her again.

"Nick?" she asked hesitantly.

"Yes, Court. Darling, that's real. We just finished loving, and I want you again already. I'll always want you. And I won't go away just because our love doesn't fit the mold you think it should. I'm going to keep asking and loving you and asking, and I'm going to convince you, Court, if it's the last thing I ever do."

Courtney's second impulse when she awoke on Sunday morning in Nick's arms was to call Julie. She waited until Monday morning to make the call from the privacy of her office because she didn't want Nick to learn what her first impulse had been. She had revealed entirely too much of her feelings to him already, and letting him know how close she was to giving in to him would be all the ammunition he would need to have her at the altar before sundown.

"Julie!" she wailed as her friend picked up the other end of the telephone and identified herself. She didn't sound the least bit like the calm, capable investments analyst she knew herself to be. She sounded like the big leap was a distinct possibility.

"Lord, Court, what's happened now?"

"I need help! Extensive psychiatric counseling! Why do I do these things to myself?"

These days, there was only one thing that made Courtney sound like an overly-excitable junior high school girl. One person, to be more precise. And since he had already moved in with her and laid claim to their baby, there was only one other thing that could have happened. . . .

"Nick's not sleeping on the sofa anymore," Julie guessed astutely.

"Why would I . . ."

"Because he's a gorgeous hunk that no woman in her right mind would keep out of her bed for long."

"But he's a . . ."

"An adorable, sweet-natured man who wants to take care of you."

"Who will destroy my career!"

"Who loves you. And wants to marry you."

"He asked again."

"You knew he would. Especially after . . ."

"I thought you were my best friend!" Courtney accused.

"I am. Which, in addition to obligating me to support you even when you're wrong, gives me the right to kick you in the butt and tell you when you're being an out-and-out idiot."

"Julie!"

"Courtney Welsch, I gave that poor man the run-around for you for weeks because I thought that was what you wanted. I called him names that my mother doesn't know I know. But you let him back into your apartment. You let him back into your life. And you let him back into your bed. Don't you dare come crying to me now, because it's obvious that you want Nick back, even if you won't admit it to yourself."

"I don't . . ."

"You do." Julie was furious and on a roll. There was no stopping her when she got like this. "Stop hiding behind this line of bull about your career. It won't be ruined, no matter what you think. If the McGuinns and Becker can't handle the idea of a professional wrestler in the family, so to speak, one of the other investment firms might be the best place for you anyway. Are you going to let four men who have no claim on you besides the fact that they're your bosses dictate your whole life? Are you going to let them pick your husband for you, for God's sake? Show a little backbone, Court!"

"Julie!"

"Is it really them, Court? Or is it you? Nick called you a snob. Are you? Are you embarrassed to admit that you're in love with a man who doesn't conform to your idea of success? Would you be acting this way if Nick were an investment banker? Or a doctor? Or a CPA?"

Nick picked up the telephone and dialed as soon as he was sure that Courtney was gone. It was early, but he wanted to make certain that he got Steve before he left the hotel for the gym. He did. From the sound of things, by lots.

" 'Lo?" a sleepy voice croaked through the telephone wires. Nick only recognized it because he had heard it hundreds of times in the last fifteen years.

"Steve? Hey, buddy, it's Nick."

"Nick?" A sniff and a heavy yawn followed. "What time is it?"

"Almost eight."

"In the morning?" Steve's voice rose incredulously.

"Yep. Got a partner for Boston yet?"

" 'S two nights."

"I know. That's okay."

"Giving up already?"

"Not a chance. Just giving Courtney some breathing space."

More awake now, Steve recognized the discrepancy between Nick's vow to stay with Courtney and his announcement that he intended to leave town for a few days. "Living in her back pocket for a couple of weeks isn't making her cave, so you're trying something else?"

"Not exactly. But the progress I'm making here is of the two-steps-forward, one-step-back variety. I'm hoping getting out of town for a few days will give her some time to think and maybe break what's becoming a pattern."

"Or maybe you just want to sleep in a real bed for a change. That couch must get real uncomfortable after a while."

"Steve . . ." Nick growled threateningly.

Steve could tell that his probing had hit a nerve. "Two steps forward, one step backward," he repeated to himself. He thought about his distinct impression that they had interrupted something when they had shown up at Courtney's apartment unannounced on Friday night. Which meant . . .

"The couch is history."

"Steve . . ." Of course he'd make the connection. The man had sex on the brain.

"And she still won't marry you? What's wrong with that woman? Or what's wrong with you that I don't know about? I never heard any complaints from any of your other ladies. At any rate, I was never able to steal any of them away from you."

"Just drop it, Steve." He was his best friend, but sometimes his mind was definitely in the sewer. "Are you working with Greg in Boston?"

"Not a chance. He's out until after Labor Day, probably."

"What?" He'd looked fine after Saturday's match.

"You didn't hear? Saturday night, Greg went down to the Village and picked up some really interesting babe." His voice told Nick plainly that "really interesting" wasn't a compliment. "Turns out the girl's into knives. She cut him, robbed him, and then left him in his hotel room. Finally, he crawled out into the corridor, and that's where Marty found him. The two of them spent most of the night in the emergency room while the doctors sewed him back together. He's not going to be a pretty sight, but he's damned lucky to be alive and functioning after this. The only thing that saved him from singing soprano was the metal zipper in his jeans."

Nick blanched at the thought, as any male would. "Jake doesn't have anybody else for you?"

"Not as far as I'm concerned. Not if you can be there. You know that, Nicky. We're leaving tonight, though."

Nick didn't hesitate. "What time?"

When Courtney arrived at her apartment that evening, Nick was gone. So was his suitcase. And the things that he kept in the bathroom, like his toothbrush, shaving supplies, and deodorant. Their collective absence could only mean one thing; he had gone considerably farther than the grocery store.

She had repeatedly insisted to Nick that she wanted him out of her apartment and her life. Now that he appeared to have acceded to her demands, however, she wasn't sure that it was what she had wanted at all. It had never occurred to her that his sudden disappearance would disrupt her life every bit as much as his abrupt re-appearance in it had done. The apartment seemed empty without him in the kitchen, a beer in his hand, watching "Live at Five" as he cooked them yet another spectacular dinner. She felt so abandoned, bereft, lost without him. She wasn't sure which disturbed her more: not having Nick there or not liking not having Nick there.

Closer inspection of the apartment revealed that Nick wasn't gone for good. His most cherished possession, his leather jacket, still hung in her bedroom closet. While it was conceivable that he might have left other clothes behind, Nick would never have left his jacket unless he intended to come back for it. Other small hints of Nick's intent to return were scattered around the apartment: his battered, paint-spattered running shoes, the second and third volumes of the science-fiction trilogy he had just begun, his Matchbox car collection, and a note on the front of the refrigerator.

A note on the refrigerator! She couldn't decide whether to be relieved, or furious, or hurt that he had left her a note instead of saying good-bye. She pulled the piece of paper off the door and unfolded it. It appeared to have been written in a hurry and didn't make a lot of sense.

Court, darling,

I'm sorry I couldn't say good-bye to you before I left, but everything came up pretty fast and I had to run to catch the plane to Boston with Steve. I'll explain everything when I call you later tonight. I'll tell you where we're staying then, too.

I called and cancelled delivery of the rest of the baby's furniture until sometime next week. I also postponed your doctor's appointment until Friday, so I can go with you. I'll be back in time to go to Lamaze on class Thursday.

Dinner for the nights I'll be gone is in the fridge. Just follow the directions on each package. Please rinse the dishes and stack them in the dishwasher, or they'll be petrified by the time I get back. Please eat the meals I made and don't send out for pizza. Don't forget your vitamins. Do your exercises. And take care of yourself and the baby.

> I love you,
> Nick

When she finished reading the note, Courtney was thoroughly confused. It sounded as if Nick had been busy before he left. Obviously, he would have had time to call her, if only he'd taken the time. What did it mean that he hadn't? Did it mean anything at all?

Sighing, she opened the refrigerator door and pulled out the first labeled dish. Since she wasn't going to get any answers until Nick called, she might as well eat dinner.

"Court, sweetheart?" The familiar, deep baritone carrying through the telephone lines sent shivers up Courtney's spine.

"Nick?" It was a silly question. He'd said he'd call, and she couldn't possibly forget that voice. She hadn't been able to since she'd heard it that first time so long ago.

"Is there someone else who calls you 'sweetheart'?" Nick grinned, even though he knew she couldn't see it.

She knew it was absurd, but she could have sworn that she heard him grin. "Nick, what on earth are you doing in Boston?"

"I wasn't supposed to be here. Greg was supposed to work with Steve in Boston." He paused, inhaling deeply before he explained the circumstances that had called him away. He didn't really want to tell her because he knew she'd think the worst of him, his friends, and wrestling in general once she heard. Less than the truth wouldn't satisfy her, though, he knew. "Saturday night, after the match, he picked up some girl in the Village and she knifed him."

"Dear God!" Courtney sounded every bit as horrified as Nick had feared she would be. "How is he?"

He was so immensely relieved that she was more concerned about Greg than the seaminess of the situation, he dared to tell her details. "Not good, but it could have been worse. She tried to castrate him, and damn near succeeded. He's sore, scared, and grateful all at the same time."

"Did they get her?" The New Yorker in her demanded justice, or at least revenge.

"No. Don't expect to, either, since Marty and Jake talked the doctor out of filing a police report."

"What?" Her voice rose incredulously.

"Court, we don't need publicity about one of the wrestlers getting stabbed and robbed. To say nothing about him cruising the bars picking up strange women."

"But . . ."

"Sweetheart, think how bad it'd look in Topeka. It doesn't exactly reinforce the image of clean, wholesome family fun."

"But just letting that woman roam the streets!"

"It's not as if this woman is stabbing innocent pedestrians out on Fifth Avenue." He didn't know how to explain it to her without sounding as if he endorsed, and possibly had participated in, such aberrant activities. Bravely, he forged ahead, making a desperate attempt to convey that he only knew about it third hand. "Court, men like Greg know there are kooks out there. They know they're taking chances every time they pick someone up. They make the choice to take that chance. For some of them, it's part of the thrill."

"Like Steve?" She made the leap that he hadn't wanted her to make, linking him, if only indirectly.

"Steve's never been quite that indiscriminate, and this has scared the hell out of him. He's not stupid, and he doesn't have a death wish." He paused and then added, emphasizing each word, "I told you before that I was never like Steve. It goes without saying that I was never like Greg, either.''

"I know, Nick. It just frightens me sometimes. Some of your friends are so . . .'' She stopped speaking because she knew there was no point in going on. He couldn't hear her anyway, over the loud, bickering, and apparently drunken voices whose owners had just entered the room. There was a struggle for the telephone receiver on Nick's end of the line. At last, another deep voice, the apparent victor, carried through to her.

"Court, it's Khalid. How are you doing, kiddo? Holding up all right?'' He was more than a little drunk, but his voice was a balm to her frayed nerves. The memory of him sitting in her living room, showing her pictures of his son while Selena looked on lovingly, injected a note of normalcy into the atmosphere of decadence and deviancy that she had constructed mentally.

"I'll be fine, Khalid,'' she assured him. "It was just a bit of a shock when I got home and he was gone.''

"And more of a shock to hear why, right?'' he added knowingly. "Nick's been tearing around like a lunatic since we got here, worrying about what you'd think when he told you.''

"Should he?''

"Court, that's not fair, convicting him by association. You know Nick better than that. He's not like that, never has been, no more than I am. Court, all wrestlers aren't like Greg. Has Nick ever shown any really kinky tendencies?'' He didn't wait for an answer. "No, don't answer that. I really don't want to know what Nick does in bed. But I've known him long enough to know that he's not into weird anymore than I am. And he's not stupid. And to get involved with a scene like where Greg found that girl is definitely weird and stupid.''

Khalid's last statement was so vague that it made Courtney wonder exactly where Greg had met his attacker and what he had intended to do with her. She didn't ask, however, because she suspected the truth would embarrass her.

"Greg's been running on the edge for a long time, Court. If he'd used half the brains God gave him, it would have occurred to him how dangerous it was. Instead, he started to believe his PR man, thought he was invincible, and did everything in his power to test that theory. It took a while, but one little girl with a knife proved how wrong he was." The contempt was plain in his voice, making it clear that Greg wasn't going to get a whole lot of sympathy from Khalid.

"I've never believed my publicity. The flash and the glitter and the girls . . . those are for the rock-star types, not guys like me. I'm not saying it was easy to avoid the lunacy; it wasn't. But I never wanted it. It's just a job to me. I do it, and then I go home to my real life. All I ever wanted were the same things that everybody else I know outside wrestling has: a wife and a kid and a house with a mortgage and a station wagon. I'm basically a normal, boring guy, and Nick's just like me."

Boring? The one thing she had never considered Nick was boring, before *or* after she knew what he did for a living.

"Court? You still there?" She hadn't spoken in so long that he wasn't sure.

"Yes," she choked.

"Maybe I stepped out of line, saying what I did." His concern sounded as sincere as his explanation had. "But I know how hard things were for Selena and me, and how much I wished that there was somebody to talk to her and tell her what I just told you."

"I know . . ." she forced out.

"Court, don't cry . . ."

The telephone was wrested out of his hand and she heard Nick's voice again.

"Court, honey, are you crying?"

"Yes," she sobbed.

"Oh, Court . . ." He wished he were in New York right now so that he could hold her and comfort her. He should never have come to Boston. ". . . please don't."

"I'll be all right." She didn't sound as if she would.

"Come to Boston, Court. Just go out to Newark and get on a plane and come," he begged.

"I can't . . ." she wailed.

"Tell Peter McGuinn to shove his job and come to me, Court."

"I'm under subpoena! I can't leave the state!"

He swore profoundly. "I'm sorry, Court, I forgot!"

"Come home, Nick."

He sighed and swore again. "I can't, sweetheart. Tomorrow . . ." His voice faded as he spoke to Khalid, but she could still hear him. "What time is it?"

She couldn't hear Khalid's answer, but she heard Steve's protest loud and clear. "What the hell are you doing, Nick?"

"I'll be back tomorrow, Steve. In plenty of time. So just don't worry about me!" Nick growled. His voice went soft and caring as he spoke into the telephone again. "Court? Sweetheart?"

"Yes, Nick?"

"I'll be there by midnight latest."

"Nick, what are you doing?"

"Coming to spend the night with you."

NINE

Courtney didn't know how Nick did it, but he was there by eleven. It wasn't important; all that mattered was that he was there. Dropping his overnight bag just inside the door, he took her in his arms and carried her to the sofa.

"I missed you so much, sweetheart," he murmured, burying his face in her hair. She smelled so good, almondy and fresh.

"I missed you, too. I was so upset when I came home and you weren't here."

"Oh, Court, I'm sorry. I should have called and told you I was going. I shouldn't have gone," he amended. Which was why he had taken the first shuttle out of Boston, in spite of the fact that helicopters and small planes terrified him. Courtney's anxiety terrified him more.

"You have to go back tomorrow?"

Nick nodded unhappily, cupped her cheeks with his palms, and looked deeply into her violet eyes. "I don't want to."

"I know." Courtney traced his lips with her finger and whispered, "I wish you didn't have to go."

"It's only until Thursday. And I'll miss you every minute that I'm gone." Groaning, he held her to him more tightly and lowered his head to capture her lips with his. "And we'll have to take full advantage of every minute until I leave."

Much later, they snuggled together in bed, spent and satisfied, and whispered in the dark. Sleep tried to claim their exhausted bodies, but both fought against it; neither wanted to waste any more of their precious time together than was absolutely necessary. The following night, when Nick was back in Boston, they could both sleep.

"Court, I won't be able to leave you after the baby's born. You know that, don't you?" His arms tightened possessively just at the thought. "If we both went off the deep end over a couple of nights apart, we'll never be able to stand a lifetime of it."

"I know," she answered softly. "I love you too much, Nick."

"Enough to marry me?" he ventured.

She shook her head silently, tears rising in her eyes.

"Enough to let me stay?"

"You mean move in with me?"

"Yes, Court, darling. Permanently."

"You already have."

"No, sweetheart, I've just been visiting. I'm talking about moving in everything I own. Finding a bigger place for us next year, maybe even a house. Buying furniture together. Getting a joint checking account. Raising our baby together. All the things couples do when they make it permanent. Court, I want you to see something."

"What?"

Without explanation, he leaned over the side of the bed, fished a piece of paper out of the pocket of his jeans, and handed it to her.

She read it. Twice. And didn't understand. "What is this?"

"Today, before I went to Boston, I made you beneficiary of my life insurance policy."

She stared at him, her puzzlement plain on her face. She obviously didn't understand the significance of the gesture.

"Where I come from, a man puts the name of the person he expects to bury him on his life insurance . . ." he began to explain.

"Nick, that's morbid! Don't talk about it! Please don't talk about it!" she cried before she used the oldest method known to woman to change the subject.

The following morning, Courtney sat at her desk, staring at the photocopy on its surface. She hadn't had a chance that morning to ask him what it was supposed to mean because they'd gotten up so late that she barely had time to get dressed and get to the office on time. And by now, she was sure that Nick had left to go back to Boston. Laying it aside with a puzzled frown, she promised herself to ask about it when he called that night.

Maggie came into the office, bearing the steadily-growing file of information that she had compiled for the grand jury's investigation about the insider trading case. Disgustedly, Courtney considered the amount of time she had been forced to spend on it. More than she had when she was still working for the guy, and she wasn't getting paid for any of it, she grumbled to herself. To say nothing of the fact that she wasn't completely cleared yet.

"I hate to be the one to have to tell you this," Maggie began hesitantly, "but Peter McGuinn wants a summary of this mess before the partners' meeting."

Groaning, Courtney rolled her eyes heavenward, pleading for mercy. There went her whole morning!

"And then, at two this afternoon, they want you to meet with Tanner and the DA." Tanner was the firm's attorney. Spending the afternoon with him would be like going to the dentist and being audited by the IRS all in the same day.

The two women spent, as Courtney had predicted, the rest of the morning plowing through the mountain of paper. At last they were finished and Maggie stood, gathering the file back together before she went out to her own office to type up the summary. She paused when she found the photocopied sheet that didn't belong. With the self-assuredness of a long-time secretary whose boss has no secrets from her, she read it, and then looked up to stare at Courtney in confusion.

" 'Nicholas Anthony Trielo,' " she said. "That's that great big fellow that plowed through here a couple of weeks ago, isn't it?"

Courtney grabbed for the paper, but Maggie held it out of her reach. "Maggie, you give that to me!"

"Not until you tell me what's going on. Who is he, Courtney, and why is he signing his life insurance over to you?"

"You're my secretary, not my mother! Give that back!"

Maggie's eyes went wide at Courtney's fevered response. She had never seen Courtney so agitated, not since the day that Mr. Trielo had come to the office. Twice. The mother in her figured it out before she could blink.

"He's the father," she realized aloud. "The father of your baby. That business about artificial insemination was just to throw everybody off the trail."

Gulping, Courtney nodded, appalled by how quickly Maggie put together the pieces.

"He didn't know about the baby until that day. That's why he looked shell-shocked when he left here."

Courtney closed her eyes and nodded again silently. She could always count on Maggie to recognize the obvious.

"Courtney Welsch, you need a keeper! This is what your friend Julie's been so worked up about ever since you found out you were pregnant! You met him on that ski trip, didn't you?"

Another reluctant nod, accompanied by a grimace on Courtney's face.

"So where is he now?" Maggie demanded. "Why aren't the two of you getting married?"

Courtney opened her mouth and shut it again. Several times. No sound emerged.

"It's obvious he loves you! If he didn't, he wouldn't have done this!" Maggie waved the piece of paper.

Courtney peered at her secretary with the same puzzled expression she had directed at Nick the night before. The significance of Nick's life insurance made no more sense to her now than it had then.

"What?" she finally choked out.

"Life insurance!" Maggie rolled her eyes in exasperation. "Lord, Courtney, how can a bright woman like you be so dense? A man only makes you the beneficiary of his life insurance when he expects you to be the one to bury him!"

"He said that when he gave this to me . . ." Courtney admitted, a pained expression on her face.

"That means he expects to be with you for the rest of his life!"

"Nick?" she asked that night when he called. "Exactly what did you mean last night when you gave me that paper?"

"Signing over my insurance to you? What do you think it means, Court?" He'd been stunned that she hadn't understood the significance of it.

"Maggie says that it means you expect to spend the rest of your life with me."

"Maggie is a very astute woman. Remind me to send her flowers."

"But, Nick . . ."

"Sweetheart, it's a commitment. Not like marriage, but a commitment all the same."

"I won't marry you, Nick."

"So you've told me. More times than I'd care to discuss or remember. But even if you never marry me, sweet heart," he said firmly, praying he wasn't tempting fate by voicing the thought aloud, "I intend to spend the rest of my life loving you."

Later that night, Courtney's telephone rang again. Sighing, resigned but not happy about it, she picked up the receiver. "Hello?"

"Court, honey, I miss you." It was Nick again. This time he sounded as if he had company and had been drinking.

"Nick, are you drunk?"

"Not yet, but we're working on it."

"We?"

"Khalid, Steve, and me. I miss you, Court."

She smiled gently and shook her head. "I miss you, too, Nick."

"Enough to marry me?"

"No, Nick."

"Damn." He sighed heavily. "It was worth a shot."

"You can't say you didn't give it the old college try."

"College try," he repeated blearily. Without warning, he began singing what Courtney suspected was the Cornell *alma mater*. In the background, Steve joined him shortly afterward.

"Nick? Nick?" she called into the telephone, trying to get his attention.

Finally, he stopped singing. "Yes, darling?"

"Was there something you called for?"

"Oh." He sighed again. "I needed to hear your voice. And I wanted to talk to the baby."

She couldn't have heard him correctly, she just knew it. "What?"

"Hold the telephone to your stomach, Court. Please?"

"You've got to be . . ."

"Please, Court?"

"Oh, for God's . . ."

"I know I'll be home tomorrow night, but I can't wait, Court. I have to talk to him."

At last, knowing that the only way she was going to get off the telephone was by humoring him, she agreed. "All right, Nick. I'll let you talk to the baby." She had absolutely no intention of doing anything so ludicrous.

There was silence on the other end of the phone for a moment, until he said, "You're not doing it."

"Of course not, Nick!"

"Selena used to do it for Khalid. He was just telling us that every night that he was on the road while she was pregnant, she used to let him talk to the baby. And I want talk to the baby. Please, Courtney?"

Exasperated, she lowered the telephone receiver to her belly. Through it, she could hear Nick's low voice, although she only understood every third word or so. She wasn't sure, but she thought he was trying to coerce their unborn child into convincing her to marry him. He went on for quite a long time before he lapsed into silence. Then, she heard her name, spoken more loudly. If she'd still had the telephone at her ear instead of her stomach, the volume would have been painful.

"Yes, Nick?" she answered, speaking into the telephone again.

"Court, love, thank you. I feel better now." His words were slower, more slurred than they had been at the beginning of their telephone conversation. "I'll see the both of you tomorrow. We have a date for Lamaze, right?"

"Right, Nick."

"I love you, sweetheart."

"I love you, too."

"One more thing, Court?"

"What's that, Nick?"

"Repeat after me: 'I love you, darling.' You've never called me 'darling' and I want to hear you say it just once."

"I love you, darling."

"Thanks, sweetheart. You've just made me the happiest man in Boston. Maybe in Massachusetts."

* * *

For the first time in the seven years she had worked for the Brothers McGuinn and Becker, Courtney left the office a full hour early, with Maggie's wholehearted blessing and a promise to cover for her if anyone were looking for her. Nick was coming home, and she wanted the extra hour with him before they went to Lamaze class.

She opened her apartment door and noticed at once that it felt like home again. The luscious smell of Trielo's special tomato sauce wafted out to the front hall from the kitchen. David Bowie sang, too loudly, about "Modern Love." Her shoes and mislaid laundry had vanished from the living room. Nick was back.

"Nick!" Courtney crowed happily, dropping her briefcase and kicking off her shoes as she raced through the apartment to the kitchen.

He grinned, opening his arms wide to receive her. She rushed into them and they closed around her in a tight hug.

Not for the first time, Courtney wondered at the range of sensations that assailed her when she was in Nick's arms. The protection provided by his size and strength always overwhelmed her, as did his uncanny ability to know exactly how and where to touch her to send sizzling electric tingles through her. Only he could instill in her such safe security and such incredible arousal simultaneously.

Stroking her back, Nick thought again about how right Courtney felt in his arms. She was so tiny and vulnerable and at the same time so fundamentally female and seductive that he didn't know whether he wanted to protect her, or throw her over his shoulder and carry her away to a cave somewhere. Compromising somewhere in the middle, he captured her lips in a tender kiss.

"Mmm," she purred against his lips. "You taste so good, like white wine."

"It's the only way you're gonna get any these days, lady," he teased.

"I know . . ." she sighed. "There are days that I could really use a glass of wine when I get home . . ." Her voice trailed as she kissed him again, more deeply. "On the other hand, maybe it tastes better this way."

His hand lifted to touch her cheek and his fingers wandered, tunnelling through her dark curls of their own accord. Moving around to cup the back of her skull, he held her head still, allowing him to take her lips at his leisure.

"Court?" he ventured.

"Hmm?" she answered, her eyes closed and her lips parted slightly.

"Do you want dinner now and dessert after class, or the other way around?"

"What's dessert?" She opened her eyes and the twin amethysts glowed up at him.

"Me," he answered in a husky whisper.

"Turn the stove off. We'll have the spaghetti after class."

"Court?" Nick knelt on the floor above Courtney's head, gently massaging her temples and neck.

"Hmm?" Her eyes closed, she breathed deeply and relaxed her abdominal muscles.

He forgot to answer her. With silent fascination, he watched the steady rise and fall of her breasts. Although it had been more than an hour since they had made love, her nipples were still tautly erect under her T-shirt. His palms tingled with the desire to take his hands from her temples and cover them.

"Nick?" Courtney asked, opening her eyes to look up at him when he didn't answer her.

"What, Court?" His gaze moved from the temptation of her breasts to her violet eyes.

"You started this, not me. Were you just checking to see if I was still awake or did you want something?"

"Yeah." He smiled down at her. "I did . . . I do. You."

"You have me, Nick." She returned his smile tremulously, hoping this conversation wasn't leading where she thought it was. Where it always led.

His hands moved down to cup her shoulders. "I mean for always, sweetheart," he said quietly, so that no one else in the class could hear him. "I don't want either of us to have any doubts that I'm yours and you're mine."

"Do you?" she evaded.

"Yeah, Court, I'm only human. I love you, darling."

"You know I love you, Nick."

"Court, I want . . . I need commitment."

"So, what's this?" She stroked her hand over the surface of her belly. "An optical illusion?"

"Court . . . you know what I mean. I need to know that you can't marry the first 'suitable' man that comes along."

That hurt. Her eyes reflected it. "You know I wouldn't do that."

"I don't know it, honey. If you won't marry me because I'm unsuitable, what's to stop you from marrying someone else because he is suitable?"

It was apparent that Nick had been agonizing about this ever since he had gone back to Boston Tuesday morning.

"I wouldn't be able to stand it, Court. As it is, I'm jealous of all the men you see at work. They're all eminently suitable."

"But I don't love them," she protested.

"As far as I can tell, sweetheart, love and marriage are totally unrelated in your mind."

Their trip to the doctor the following day only aggravated the tension between them. The woman took one look at Nick and another at Courtney, and promptly ordered another sonogram. The procedure confirmed her worst suspicions; the baby wasn't due for another two months, and she estimated its current weight at well over five and possibly six pounds. At birth, she anticipated at least eight pounds. Given Courtney's size, Lamaze was probably out of the question; in fact, the doctor had seriously discussed a Caesarian.

Nick was simultaneously depressed and panic-stricken. In spite of the vast discrepancy between their sizes, it had never occurred to him that their baby might be too big for tiny Courtney to deliver naturally. He had wanted to be there when their child was born, and every day that hope looked less and less likely as Court got bigger and bigger. Additionally, the idea of the risk involved with a Caesarian scared him half to death, as did the notion that she would come to resent him as the person responsible for the size of the baby. When he talked to her stomach, he told the baby that was already too big to stop growing.

Courtney was even less enthused with the idea of a Caesarian than Nick was. She wanted to have a baby, not a horse, she thought as she watched her stomach grow steadily larger. She had never undergone any surgery more complex than having two of her wisdom teeth removed under local anesthesia, and wasn't at all sure that she wanted her first experience with major surgery to be childbirth. Although it was both irrational and unrealistic at this late date, she had an overwhelming urge to call the whole thing off.

The hottest summer of the century plodded on entirely too slowly to suit either Courtney or Nick. She began to retain water so badly that salt became the ultimate four-letter word. Her ankles ballooned. The backs of her legs looked like a schematic map of the New York subway system. She was thoroughly miserable. She felt hot and sticky and uncomfortable, and gave serious consideration to wallowing in the bathtub like a hippo until the heat wave broke, she went into labor, or the world ended, whichever came first.

Nick did his best to comfort her, but she was so cranky

that nothing seemed to help. He made her elevate her feet every day after dinner. He told her repeatedly how beautiful she was. He made a three a.m. trip to four different stores in search of Swiss-chocolate-candy-almond ice cream. He insisted there was salt in the salt-free lasagna. He assured her that if the crib said "some assembly required," it meant that two college-educated adults could put it together.

She knew he was lying. Just like she knew he was lying when he told her that she didn't look like a beached whale. Just like she knew he was lying when he told her that the discomfort was only going to continue for another couple of weeks. She was going to have the only twelve-year pregnancy in history.

Making love was, for all intents and purposes, out of the question. The doctor had told them that it was safe for another month or so and Nick still wanted her—more than ever, as a matter of fact—but Courtney would rarely tolerate more affection than an occasional hug and quick kiss. Nick strongly suspected that her attitude toward sex was influenced by the knowledge that that was what had gotten her into this dilemma in the first place.

The weeks passed. It got hotter and more humid. Courtney got more uncomfortable and crankier. It got more and more difficult for Nick to humor her. Both of them started to look forward to his overnight trips because the day or two they spent apart gave them, first, the chance to cool down and, then, the opportunity to miss each other. By the time he returned from Philadelphia, Atlanta, or Cleveland, both were ready for the loving reconciliation that followed. A few days later, the antagonism started all over again. In spite of their best efforts, the toilet paper facing the wrong way on the spindle was enough to start World War III.

Steve, although he was Nick's best friend, wouldn't understand or be able to help. Taylor, while understanding, could offer little in the way of practical advice. And his sisters . . . well, they were utterly out of the question, because they suspected too much already. If he asked any questions at all, no matter how carefully worded, they'd know. And he had a good idea that their well-meaning help could jeopardize everything. In desperation, Nick turned to Khalid.

The two men met at the same restaurant where Nick and Steve had had lunch the previous month. When Nick arrived, Khalid was already settled in at their table, his concentration divided between a plate of fried zucchini and the *Times*. Nick reached across the table and snagged several slices as he took his seat, getting Khalid's attention. The other man grinned up at him wryly.

"Don't tell on me," he pleaded. "I love them, and Selena's watching my cholesterol now. No fried foods, no eggs, no bacon . . ."

"They have great veal here," Nick interrupted, opening his menu.

"No veal. I want red meat."

Nick laughed and shook his head. "If this is what being married is like, why do I want to do it?"

"Masochism," Khalid returned wisely, munching on another piece of zucchini. "Plain and simple."

"I never thought I had masochistic tendencies . . . until recently."

"Things are tough? Court's what . . . seven months pregnant now? In August? The hottest August of this century? She's a little cranky, right?"

"Cranky doesn't begin to cover it. She's downright bitchy." Nick summarized the way things had been for most of that month and Khalid listened, nodding and smiling knowingly now and then. By the time he was through, the smiles had turned to laughter.

"You think this is funny?" Nick demanded, affronted by the other man's reaction.

"Only because I'm not the one going through it this time."

"I think I'm gonna kill her before it's all over," Nick growled unhappily. "Not that I want to, but I may not be able to stop myself."

"Just wait until after she has the baby and can't stop crying. Then, you'll wish she'd scream."

"This is normal?"

Khalid nodded. "Absolutely. What can you expect? Her hormones are on a rampage, it's ninety-five degrees, and she's hauling around a stomach that's one-third of her total body weight. If she didn't get crazy, they'd nominate her for sainthood."

Nick looked chagrined. He should have been more understanding. He felt like the most inconsiderate cretin that had ever been born.

"To say nothing about you badgering that poor woman to marry you."

"Badgering?"

"That's exactly what you've been doing, whether or not you'll admit it."

"What am I supposed to do?" Nick hissed, trying to keep his voice down. "I love her! She's pregnant with my baby! And I want to marry her!"

"Why don't you consider letting the whole thing ride until after the baby is born?"

Nick blanched at the suggestion. "I . . ."

"What's more important? Having Court be sure about marriage or having everything proper before the baby comes?"

Nick gulped uneasily. "But now, with the baby coming, I've got leverage to convince her. Afterward . . ."

"Nick! You're thinking like your Gramma Trielo! It'll never work if you try to convince Court that you 'have to get married because she's in trouble.' "

"It sounds silly when you put it that way," Nick admitted.

"It better," Khalid muttered. "Take my advice. Wait."

"But what if she never agrees to marry me?"

"She will, sooner or later, if you'll just stop badgering her. She loves you."

Maggie made all the arrangements for lunch. She called and made a date with Julie, whom she believed was her most effective ally. Then, she called and made reservations all the way uptown at Tavern on the Green, cleared Courtney's entire afternoon of appointments, requisitioned a replacement for herself from the pool, and informed all the necessary people that she and Courtney would both be out of the office. Finally, she told her boss that she was taking her out to lunch and hustled her into a cab before she could object.

They met Julie at the restaurant. Courtney was appropriately impressed. The Tavern on the Green wasn't a place to go just because you were hungry. Going to Tavern on the Green was an event.

"Come on, you two, give," Courtney said, tapping the table in front of her with one finger. "What's up?"

"Just lunch," Maggie answered.

Both women looked at her and smiled innocently. Too innocently.

"Aren't we allowed to take you out to lunch? Or eat ourselves?" Julie asked.

"If all that was involved was food, we'd be at McDonald's right now," Courtney retorted.

"Three women who are friends can't go somewhere nice together for lunch without you getting suspicious?" Maggie opened her menu purposefully.

"Not when two of them are you and the third is me. You two are up to something," she accused.

"All right, we are," Julie admitted. "We wanted to talk to you about Nick."

Courtney groaned, closing her eyes as if it could cut off Julie's words. "Hasn't enough been said?"

"Not hardly," Maggie huffed. "Not if you love him

and he loves you and you won't marry him. Especially not now." She glanced at Courtney's stomach significantly.

"He wants to be a father," Julie argued.

"He's got his wish, then. I agreed to give him full paternal rights."

Maggie rolled her eyes heavenward. "And he wants to be with you."

"I agreed to that, too."

"For the rest of your lives!" Julie exhorted her.

Courtney felt as if she were at a tennis match, looking back and forth between the players as they exchanged vollies. "That has been ruled out."

"He wants to marry you!" Maggie hissed.

"That has been ruled out," Courtney said firmly.

"He made you beneficiary of his life insurance!" Julie ground out through clenched teeth.

Courtney's head shot back to Maggie and she glared at her. "You told!" she accused.

"She beat it out of me."

"So why won't you marry him?" Julie snarled.

"He's a . . ."

"If you say it again, I'm gonna scream at the top of my lungs!" Julie threatened. "And none of us will ever be allowed in here again for as long as we live!"

"What do you want me to say?"

"Say you'll marry that poor man!" both women begged.

"You don't have to have a big wedding or a reception," Maggie pointed out.

"You don't have to tell anybody you got married if you don't want to. Except the IRS, of course."

"You don't even have to go to City Hall. Taylor says he'll fix it all with Judge Kramer. He used to clerk for him. He can get the license, and all you'll have to do is have the blood tests and go to his office and have him marry you."

In the face of two such stubborn adversaries, Courtney had no choice. She caved. "All right. The next time Nick asks, I'll say yes."

TEN

Nick left his lunch with Khalid filled with new resolve. He knew now that Court's moodiness was perfectly normal. In fact, it was understandable. Although he had known she was uncomfortable, he had never given much thought to *how* uncomfortable she was. Nor had he considered how much he was aggravating the situation with his constant proposals.

He promised himself that, no matter how much it tore him apart, he wouldn't mention marriage again, not until after the baby was born. He hoped his self-control was up to it. More importantly, he hoped his new-found restraint would put her in a better frame of mind.

Nick was in the kitchen, peeling shrimp, when he heard the door of the apartment open and then close again. "Hon?" he called out. "I'm in here."

Courtney appeared in the doorway, looking happier than she had in days.

"You let the doctor tell you what sex the baby is?" he guessed. She had offered to tell them after the sonogram, but they had, as one, vetoed it.

"No . . ." she replied, folding her arms over her stomach. "Do you need to do that now?"

144

"Only if we want dinner. They made you a junior partner?"

She shook her head. "Not yet. They won't be voting on that until late fall."

Nick put the shrimp in the refrigerator, washed his hands, and dried them on a dish towel. His hips were propped on the edge of the counter, his long legs crossed in front of him, as he ran the cloth between his fingers. "You won a lifetime supply of Swiss-chocolate-candy-almond ice cream?"

She shook her head again and laughed. "Isn't it enough that I'm glad to see you?"

He flashed that adorable grin that melted her nail polish. "Does that mean I get a hug?"

Courtney uncrossed her arms and held them out at her sides. "That means you get anything you want."

Stepping close to her, he lifted his hand to push up her chin. "Anything?"

"Anything."

"Oh, Court . . ." he groaned as his head bent and his lips touched hers. "I want you. Can we still make love?"

Her tongue darted out to touch his lower lip. "Yes," she breathed against the wet spot she left behind.

"You're sure?"

Her arms went up to encircle his neck, she tunneled her fingers through his thick dark hair, and pulled his head down to hers.

"I guess that answers that," Nick muttered against her mouth before he captured it in a passionate kiss that muffled her reply.

"Nick?" Steve's voice carried through the telephone wires, sounding vaguely unnatural, although Nick couldn't begin to imagine why.

"It's me. What's up that couldn't wait until tonight?"

"You're a real bastard, you know that?" The attack came as a complete surprise, and Nick could tell now that the strangeness he hadn't been able to identify was pure venom.

"What?"

"You heard me, buddy, and you know exactly what I'm talking about."

Nick searched the depths of his mind and couldn't come up with anything that had happened since he had last seen Steve that would have made him this angry at him.

"That's a hell of a way to treat Court, no matter what kind of problems you two are having . . ."

Ah ha, Nick thought. It made sense. Somehow, Steve had heard that he had stopped asking Court to marry him. Obviously, he didn't understand the reasoning behind the decision. "Steve, don't go flying off the handle until I explain . . ."

"Explain? I'd say you owe the explanation to Court, not me!"

"I have no intention of telling her what I'm doing!" Nick protested.

"If you're trying to win her back, you've sure got a peculiar way of going about it . . ."

"She'd been out-of-sorts and cranky and all I did . . ."

"Nick, I don't think it would be possible to make her madder than I'm sure she is right now," Steve continued, not hearing a word of his attempted explanation. "Even if you hadn't promised, it was a real cheap thing to do, knowing how she feels about wrestling . . ."

"What are you talking about?"

Brought up short by Nick's question, Steve stumbled at the other end of the line. Finally, he asked tentatively, "You really don't know what I'm talking about, do you?"

"Haven't a clue."

"If you didn't talk to them, who did?"

"Talk to whom?"

"You haven't seen the afternoon papers yet, have you?"

Nick felt his scalp prickle and the pit of his stomach

tightened. There wasn't a legitimate afternoon paper in the city, which meant . . . "No," he breathed. "Oh, God . . ."

"I don't know how they found out, Nicky, but the news is out."

Nick closed his eyes and sank back onto the sofa sickly, too weak to support himself.

"Are you still there?"

"Yes. What does it say?"

"You want me to read it to you?"

"Please." Nick was too shaky to go out and get a paper himself.

" 'Nick Trielo, the darker half of the popular tag wrestling team known as the Brawny Buccaneers, has reportedly taken yet another series of unscheduled leaves of absence from the pro-wrestling circuit. In many recent matches, the fair-haired member of the duo, Steve Dixon, has been paired with the Rock and Roll Squad's Greg Melrose and Mike Warren, while first one and then the other was sidelined with injuries, Khalid "The Desert Fox" Abaza, and "Squeaky" Nichols.' "

So far, nothing sounded too awful. Maybe it wasn't really as bad as Steve thought it was.

" 'According to reliable sources, Dixon has no intention of waiting for Trielo to return and has already begun searching for a new partner, disgusted with Trielo's second disappearance from the ring this year. The first resulted from Trielo's skiing accident last January, which left him with a broken leg and Dixon without a partner for eight weeks.' "

"So why is this going to make Court so mad? She'd be thrilled if I gave it up for good."

"Pay attention, Nicky; we're getting to that part." He paused for full dramatic effect. " 'That interim may well be responsible for Trielo's current on-and-off retirement, as reliable sources indicate that Trielo is taking time off until paramour Courtney Welsch . . .' "

Nick groaned and felt beads of sweat break out on his forehead.

" '. . . an investments analyst, whom he met during the ill-fated ski vacation, gives birth to their child sometime this fall. Although . . .' "

"Steve," Nick choked out, "please tell me there isn't any more."

"Sorry, Nick."

"At least tell me it doesn't get any worse," Nick begged.

"Do you want me to read the rest of this to you or not?"

"Go ahead . . ."

" 'Although the couple has revealed no immediate plans to marry, Trielo has taken up residence in Welsch's fashionable West Side apartment where he is, reportedly, tending to household matters while Welsch continues to work as a senior analyst for McGuinn, McGuinn, McGuinn, and Becker . . .' "

"Steve?"

"Yes, Nick?"

"You got any ideas as to countries that'll grant me immediate asylum?"

"What for?"

"When Court lays eyes on me, she's going to kill me."

"At least the photographer got her good side. The one of you's not so great."

"Courtney?" Maggie's voice carried through the intercom, sounding entirely too harried for a late Friday afternoon. Clients rarely asked for advice that they couldn't use until after the weekend. "It's another reporter on the telephone," she hissed. "This one's from . . ."

"Just tell him no comment, Maggie. I don't know why they're all so excited about it, anyway. You'd think there was some sort of multi-million dollar fraud involved, instead of some lousy small-time . . ."

"Courtney, I don't think they're calling about that case." She hesitated and then plowed forward bravely. "This one's asking questions about you and Nick. What's going on?"

"Oh, dear God!"

"He said there was something in the afternoon papers?" Her voice rose at the end. Why anyone would care to read about Courtney and Nick was beyond her. "What do you want me to do?"

"Get rid of him and get in here with a copy of that paper, Maggie! Fast!"

Courtney told herself that she was jumping to all the wrong conclusions with nothing, really, on which to base them. All the reporter had said, according to Maggie, was that her name had been linked with Nick's in one of the scandal sheets. There were hundreds of perfectly reasonable explanations why a reporter would call her and ask about Nick that didn't have anything to do with Nick living with her or the baby. And she didn't believe one of them, not deep down inside.

Maggie was winded when she dropped into a chair across the desk from Courtney, the newspaper in question clenched in her fist.

Courtney took the tabloid from her and leafed through it frantically. The last of the color washed from her pale face as she gaped at the side-by-side photographs of herself and Nick. For a moment, she forgot how to breathe.

"Courtney, are you all right?" Maggie asked, filled with concern for her boss. She'd never seen her look worse, not even the first day that Nick had barged into her office.

Courtney took a deep breath and exhaled slowly. Bracing mentally, she forced herself to read the article. It couldn't possibly be as bad as her worst fears, she told herself before she began.

She was wrong. It was worse. Much worse. The only

thing about her that they'd left out of the article was her social security number.

"Courtney?"

Her violet eyes were saucer-wide as she forced them upward from the newspaper to meet Maggie's. Her hand shook as she handed back the section of the paper with her picture.

Maggie read the article and her head shot up. "He's a professional wrestler?" she asked incredulously.

Courtney paled even further and smiled sickly.

"What in God's name made you think you could keep a thing like this a secret?" Maggie demanded.

"I tried . . ." Courtney answered weakly.

"For crying out loud, wrestling's the hottest thing around these days! They're celebrities, like rock stars and actors! Something like this would be worth a fortune to the papers! Can you imagine what they paid for this tip?"

If it was a tip at all, Courtney thought. Nick still might have told, in a last-ditch, desperate effort to get her to marry him; after all, he didn't know that she'd decided to say yes. No, she argued with herself. He wouldn't have told. He promised. . . . But who else would have?

Maggie echoed her question. "Who else knows?"

Unable to speak, Courtney waved frantically at the newspaper that Maggie still held. Everyone in the city with basic reading skills knew now.

Maggie recognized that someone had to take charge of the situation, if only to head off the reporters and the brothers McGuinn and a possible invasion by Mr. Triel himself. She also recognized that that someone would have to be her; clearly, Courtney was in no condition to take charge of tying her shoelaces. Pulling herself up to her full height, she leaned across the desk, and raised Courtney's chin so that their eyes met.

"Courtney, you've got to buck up," she ordered in her best drill sergeant's voice. "Pull yourself together. Do you need a glass of water?"

Hiccoughing, Courtney nodded.

Maggie forced Courtney to drink the whole thing slowly. "Now, while the phones are all tied up . . ." Maggie had devised an ingenious method of blocking all the telephone lines at once, which she only used in cases of real emergency. This was, undeniably, one. ". . . you're going to have to come up with some sort of game plan . . ."

"Game plan?" Courtney echoed hollowly.

"I think we can hold off the press with 'no comment' for the rest of the day, but I don't have the slightest doubt that they're going to be waiting for you when you leave here tonight."

"Outside? Here?"

"And at your apartment building. Trust me, Courtney. I did learn something in the two years I worked for that talent agency. You're news, and they're not going to leave you alone. . . . Speaking of which, they're probably going to try to get in here. We'll have to tell the front receptionist what's going on, which, of course, means that the senior partners are going to get wind of this. I'd say you have fifteen minutes—tops—to come up with an explanation for them."

"Oh, God," Courtney groaned. "I'm going to kill myself."

"Later. You have too much to do right now."

Not for the first time that afternoon, Nick wondered how so many reporters had gotten Courtney's unlisted number. The telephone had been ringing off the hook ever since the afternoon papers had appeared on the newsstand. The only thing keeping him from unplugging the thing altogether was the likelihood that Court would call. When he did, he didn't want the phone to ring and ring with no answer because it would only make him feel guiltier than he felt already.

"Hello?" It took everything he had in him not to snarl

into the receiver until he found out whether it was Courtney or another reporter.

"Nicky?"

It couldn't be, but it was. "Yeah, it's me. Gramma,
how'd you get this phone number?"

"I got it from Lisa." He'd given the number to his
sister in case of emergency. Obviously, his family considered a newspaper article announcing his impending fatherhood emergency enough. "Nicky, what's going on? Why
won't you marry this girl?"

He could trust his little Italian grandmother to get right
to the heart of the matter. "Gramma, I asked her and she
told me no . . ."

"Then you didn't ask right. Nicky, didn't I teach you
better than this? Everyone in the neighborhood is calling
and they all want to know the same thing: 'When's Nick
going to marry this girl?' "

"Gramma, she won't marry me. I've asked her and
asked her . . ."

"And she lets you live there? What kind of girl is this
that you picked to be the mother of my great-grandchild.
She's not Italian, is she?"

"Gramma, really . . ." Nick stopped at the realization
that there was no way he was going to be able to explain
the importance of Courtney's career and her fears about
the effect his presence would have on it to the woman who
considered perfecting cannoli the greatest achievement of
her life.

"Really, nothing," she insisted. "I'll send Father Castagna to speak with her. He's a good man, and he under-
stands you young people."

"No! Gramma, don't . . ."

"Now don't you tell me don't, Nicholas. None of my
children or grandchildren have had babies without being
married, and I have no intention of letting you be the first.
I'll never hear the end of it from your Aunt Louisa and

the neighbors. You don't want to embarrass me, do you, Nicky?''

The woman was devious. He had to give her that. She knew exactly what to say to make him feel like an ungrateful, inconsiderate child. It had worked when he was four and it still worked at thirty-four. For a moment, he forgot that it was Court who wouldn't get married, not him.

"Nicky, are you listening to me?"

"Yes, Gramma, but . . ."

"But nothing, Nicky. If you won't talk reason to me, I'll just have to talk to her."

Before he could protest her intended action, she was gone. Knowing precisely what she intended to do next, Nick grabbed a T-shirt, pulling it over his head on the way out the door. He had to get across town and tell Court what had happened before the rest of the world did it for him.

"Courtney, I've got a call on hold here that I think you really ought to take."

"Who is it?" she wailed miserably. "My parents? Don't tell me the wire services have picked it up already!"

"It's a woman named Anna Trielo. Sounds older."

Obviously one of Nick's relatives, Courtney told herself, cringing inwardly. She really wasn't in a humor to deal with any Trielos, including Nick, at the moment. But then again, she ought to take it. Torn between cowardice and duty, she didn't know what to do.

"Courtney," Maggie, now acting as voice of conscience, added, "you know that you ought to take the call."

"You're right, Maggie," she answered, knowing full well that it was true. "Put her through."

"Good girl," Maggie praised. Somehow, it made her feel more like a puppy that had just fetched a stick than a successful executive who had just reached a decision.

"Hello? Mrs. Trielo?" Courtney said into the receiver.

"Is this Courtney Welsch?" The voice that answered her was older, as Maggie had said, and had a pronounced Italian accent.

"Yes, it is," Courtney assured her.

"You're that girl that won't marry my Nicky?"

Oh, Lord, Courtney thought, feeling slightly sick. She already felt worse than she had when she had seen the newspaper. Mrs. Trielo had a way of making it sound as if Nick were the one "in trouble" instead of her.

"Well, are you?" the tiny voice laced with steel demanded.

"Yes," Courtney admitted reluctantly. She wondered i Italians had curses like gypsies.

Apparently they did, because a long, drawn-out stream of Italian carried through the telephone wires to her. She didn't understand a word of it. She didn't need to. The tone of voice communicated Mrs. Trielo's opinion of the matter.

At last, the tirade lapsed back into English. "If you don't marry my Nicky, the baby won't have a name!"

Courtney elected to fight high emotion with logic. "The baby will most certainly have a name, Mrs. Trielo. Nic and I have already talked about it, and we agreed t hyphenate . . ."

"Hyphenate?"

"Put our names together, like Trielo-Welsch," Cour ney explained.

"No!" She went back to hysterical Italian again.

Courtney sighed wearily and continued with logic, i spite of the fact that it had proven totally ineffectiv already. "And you don't have to worry about never seein the baby because we've agreed . . ."

"Like divorced people?" The question left no doubt Courtney's mind that this was not the time to disclose th she had agreed to continue living with him after the bat was born. The woman was already aghast. "No one our family has ever been divorced . . . Even cousin Lucia, and her Gino drank too much . . .''

Courtney harbored a sneaking suspicion that cousin Lucia should have taken the chance and horrified the family. Exercising prudence, she kept that thought to herself.

"And none of our babies have been born out of wedlock . . . To think that my grandson Nicky's baby would be the first . . . it shames me. We'll make a nice wedding for you, just like we did for my sister Louisa's girl when she was expecting Joey . . .''

Courtney bit her tongue, preventing herself from offering the opinion that Joey's father should have had the sense to head for Canada the minute the Trielo clan came after him. And she should have followed him.

Gasping for breath, Nick loomed over Maggie's desk, leaning one big hand on it for support while the other clutched at a cramp in his side. After his cab had gotten stuck in traffic, he'd gotten out and run the last twelve blocks to Courtney's office.

With consummate serenity that belied the chaos of the last hour and negated all the appearances that he was a madman, Maggie looked up at Nick. "Yes?"

His mouth worked frantically, but he couldn't summon the oxygen necessary for words.

Levelly, Maggie asked, "Do you know a woman named Anna Trielo?"

His eyes rolled wildly as he forced out, "Oh, Lord, no! Please tell me she hasn't called Court yet!"

Maggie glanced down and checked the light on the telephone. "They're still on the telephone."

Turning, Nick burst through the door and into the office, snatching the telephone receiver from an astonished Courtney. "Gramma, what do you think you're doing?"

"Helping, Nicky . . ."

"Gramma, you're not helping. You're interfering. I want you to hang up that phone this instant . . .''

"I talked to Father Castagna. He says that she wouldn't have to convert." She sighed heavily. "Although it would be nice to have my great-grandchild be raised Roman Catholic . . ."

"Gramma, please . . . not now! I'll call you, I promise . . ."

"Will you bring her for manicotti on Sunday?"

Nick rolled his eyes heavenward and begged for intervention. "I'll see, Gramma. Let me talk to her. I'll call you back."

She sniffed, as if bearing the burdens of the world on her shoulders. "Fine, Nicky. You know where to find me . . ."

He certainly did. She'd lived in the same house for fifty years and he couldn't remember the last time she'd made the trek from Brooklyn to Manhattan. "Good-bye, Gramma."

Hanging up the telephone, Nick turned to look at Court. She was so pale that it frightened him. "Court, I'm so sorry, honey. . . . I never thought she'd call you, especially not here . . ."

"What the hell is going on, Nick?" she demanded, waving the newspaper at him, so angry that she was quivering. "How did they find out?"

He shook his head helplessly. "I don't know, honey. . . ." There was no point in telling her that, from some of the things in the article, he had concluded that there had been a reporter in the restaurant where he and Khalid had had lunch the day before.

"You didn't tell?" she asked, her eyes narrowed with suspicion.

"And bring Gramma Trielo down on you intentionally? Courtney, really!"

Courtney flung the newspaper down on the desk and sank into her chair. "So what am I supposed to do now?"

Nick contemplated the unspoken implications of the question. The reporters were outside, hovering like vultures. "No comment" wasn't going to get them out of the building. It was too late to forestall any damage this would do to her career. And only the East River separated them from Gramma Trielo and a shotgun wedding. All things considered, there was only one solution. . . .

"Marry me."

ELEVEN

During the long months between April and August, Nick had said those words so many times that he couldn't begin to guess how many times he'd repeated them. He had tried everything ... tenderly romantic proposals accompanied by moonlight and roses, feverishly impassioned pleas whispered in bed, endearingly sweet entreaties delivered by the U.S. postal system and FTD, even shouted demands made in the heat of anger. None of them had accomplished its intended purpose. Time after time, she had refused to marry him.

Now, in an office held under siege by the triple threats of eager reporters, imminent invasion by her employers, and the lingering wrathful spirit of Gramma Trielo, Courtney said yes.

Nick gaped at her. *Now?* he asked himself incredulously. *Now, she says yes?* He couldn't have contrived a more prosaic setting and proposal if he'd tried. He'd made getting married sound about as desirable and romantic as a trip to the laundromat. And she'd accepted.

He'd expected to be thrilled when she finally agreed to marry him. At the very least, he'd expected to be pleased. Instead, he felt a vague sense of letdown and disconten that an eavesdropping reporter had managed to accomplish what he had been attempting for months. He didn't want her to marry him because she felt trapped and couldn't see any other way out. Damn it, he wanted her to marry him because she loved him and wanted to spend the rest of her life with him! He frowned at the thought.

Courtney peered curiously at Nick. For months, he'd been asking her to marry him. Now, she'd said yes, and the only word she could use to describe the expression on his face was annoyed. There was no figuring the man.

He had known all along that only her fears about possible repercussions in her career had kept her from agreeing to marriage. The article in that day's paper had sent that obstacle flying out the window. It was much too late for secrecy. The McGuinns and Becker were going to find out about Nick and there was nothing she could do to forestall the potential damage. With that out of the way, there was only the reality that Nick made her happier than she'd ever been in her life. Now, there was no reason not to marry him.

She'd just expected him to be more . . . enthusiastic about it.

He continued to frown at her. "Why, Court?"

She blinked in confusion, not understanding. "Why what?"

"Why now? Why are you saying yes? You've been telling me for months that you wouldn't . . . couldn't marry me. And all of a sudden . . . poof!" He threw up his hands dramatically. "You say yes."

"You didn't want me to?"

He sighed deeply and slumped his head against the back of the chair. "Of course, I did . . . I kept asking you, didn't I?"

"Until you were blue in the face."

"But I wanted you to say yes because you love me, not because some reporter found out about us and the baby." His voice was filled with despair.

"But I do love you. You know that, Nick."

He raised his head and looked levelly at her. "Do I?"

The question hurt. Courtney closed her eyes and gulped back the threat of tears.

"Oh, God, Court, I'm sorry," Nick apologized, bolting out of his chair and rushing toward her. He hadn't meant to make her cry. These days, a couple of tears had a tendency to degenerate into a deluge; besides, he didn't want her to remember that he had made her cry immediately after she had agreed to marry him. "I didn't mean it. It just came as such a shock for you to say yes now. I had . . ."

". . . given up on getting me to say it?" she completed for him, looking up at him through glistening violet eyes.

He hugged her tightly. "Court, I've never given up. It's what I've wanted all along. I love you, sweetheart."

It took one of Maggie's best efforts to get Nick and Courtney out of the building without encountering any of the McGuinns, Becker, or the reporters. Smoothly, efficiently, in the same manner that she accomplished everything, she arranged for a cab, guided them out of the building via a convoluted route known only to her, the janitors, and the architects who designed the building, and hustled them into the waiting vehicle, skillfully eluding the reporters skulking outside the service entrance. As she slammed the car door behind them, she confidently assured them that similar evasive maneuvers would be undertaken if she were confronted by their employers.

As the cab pulled away from the curb, Courtney covered her eyes with one hand and moaned miserably.

Nick slid his arm around the vague remnant of her waist and stroked her side in comfort. "You feeling okay?" he asked nervously.

She nodded and sighed. "As well as can be expected at this point. I have a headache."

His hand slipped up her back and began to massage the

tight muscles at her nape. "C'mon, sweetheart, relax. It's not gonna be so bad being married to me, is it?"

"It's not that, Nick. Not in my wildest imaginings did I ever expect that getting married would have any relation whatsoever to nosy reporters and photographers and cursing Italian grandmothers and . . ."

"My grandmother cursed you?"

"How should I know? I don't speak Italian."

"She was cursing," he confirmed.

"And I never expected getting married to have anything to do with sneaking out of my office so my boss doesn't find me and, God knows, I never expected to be . . ."

"Expecting?" he offered helpfully.

She glared at him, unamused. "At my age!"

"Court, it happens . . ."

"Not to responsible grown-ups, it doesn't! The year we were fifteen, I failed gym and Jenny Christwell got herself . . ."

"Who's Jenny Christwell?" A beat later, incredulously, "You failed gym?"

"Forget about the gym, Nick; it's not important. Anyway, Jenny and I were friends in high school. She got herself in trouble and had to get married the same year I failed gym. And here I am, fifteen years later, getting myself in trouble and having to get married. What is this, Nick? Delayed development?"

"Oh, honey . . ." he groaned as he pressed a kiss to her temple. "Don't do this to yourself. We took all the right precautions . . . it just didn't work. It happens that way sometimes . . ."

"Just like a couple of damned stupid fifteen year olds, Nick!"

"No, we're not, Court," Nick insisted, cupping her cheek with his hand and turning her head so that she faced him. "There's one very big difference here. We're not kids. We're ready to handle it. Emotionally, mentally, financially. . . . And anyway, Court, I can't say I'm sorry it happened. I'm excited about the baby. I think . . ."

"The meter's still runnin', buddy," the cab driver interrupted. "And we're there. If you wanna sit back there and argue, that's your business, but . . ."

Nick nodded his acknowledgement and reached across Courtney's stomach to open the door for her. "C'mon, sweetheart, let's go up to the apartment and discuss this." He gave her a much-needed boost from behind and then followed her out onto the sidewalk. Once there, he handed the money to the cabbie and turned toward the building. Out of the corner of his eye, he caught sight of several members of the media launching a surprise flank attack. Muttering several choice profanities, Nick put his arm around Courtney and propelled her into the building. He sighed with relief as the elevator door slid shut behind them, leaving the doorman to contend with the pursuing horde.

"Court, darling, I've got a great idea. Let's just get married. Tomorrow's Saturday. We'll get Julie and Taylor on the phone tonight, drive up to Rhode Island first thing in the morning, and just get married. No fuss, no fanfare, no foolishness."

The telephone was ringing when they opened the door to the apartment.

"Nicky, why didn't you tell us what was going on?" Nick's sister Lisa demanded petulantly as soon as he picked it up. "You've been calling all of us for household hints all this time . . . we should have known something was up."

"Hello, Lisa. It's nice to talk to you, too."

"When Gramma read it, she was so upset that she had two glasses of Chianti."

That explained the tenor of her telephone call to Courtney. Anna Trielo had one glass of Chianti when she was notified of a death in the family. Two meant that she considered the discovery of Nick's impending unwed fatherhood a crisis of colossal magnitude. "She shouldn't have called Court, Lisa."

"Of course she should have! We're talking about the first Trielo great-grandchild!"

It wasn't Anna Trielo's first great-grandchild. She had fifteen. "You and Gina and . . ."

"But they're not Trielos! They all have other last names!"

"You could have hyphen . . ." Nick began.

"Don't start that again, Nick! It nearly gave Gramma an attack!"

In all the years of her threatened attacks, Nick had never been able to determine attacks of what. "For God's sake, Lisa . . ." He took a deep, calming breath. "Lisa, look, we just got into the apartment. We haven't even had a chance to sit down yet. I'll call you back later after we figure out what we're doing . . ."

"What do you mean, figure out what you're doing? You're getting married . . ."

Nick hung up on his sister before she could say any more. Even as he did so, he knew he hadn't heard the last of it. Not by a long shot. There was still his mother to be heard from. And Gina, Toni, and Marie, his three other sisters. And Father Castagna. And possibly the Pope.

Courtney tried to take a nap before dinner because Nick insisted that she do so. She suspected that he had an ulterior motive, removing her from the telephone, allowing him the opportunity to screen all calls. The instrument's persistent ringing thwarted all her efforts to sleep and, finally, she emerged from the bedroom, just in time to answer it as it rang again.

"Yes?" she snapped into the mouthpiece.

"Is this Courtney Welsch?"

She didn't recognize the male voice, but it was apparent that, whoever it was, he didn't know her either. Another reporter, she thought disgustedly. She was going to have to get her number changed again. "Who's this?"

"I'm Father Anthony Castagna, from St. Cecelia's in Brooklyn. Anna Trielo called me earlier today about wedding arrangements for her grandson and you."

Courtney paled, stunned. Gramma Trielo had already called the priest! As if that weren't bad enough, she had snarled at him! "I . . . I'm sorry, Father. I didn't mean to . . . snap at you, but the phone's been ringing off the hook with reporters and . . ."

He chuckled lowly, and she felt better about it. "I understand completely. I'm sure it's been a circus since the newspapers came out this afternoon."

"It has been," she admitted.

"Well, then, as I told Mrs. Trielo, the sanctuary is free at noon on the third Saturday in September. That gives us three Sundays to read the banns before the wedding. We won't have time for the two of you to attend the full premarital counseling course, but I believe that we can work around that. . . . I could meet with both of you individually between now and the wedding. It's a bit irregular, but you're both older, so I'm not terribly concerned about it. . . ."

Courtney's head reeled and she was stunned into silence. Banns? Pre-marital counseling? What had happened to going to Rhode Island tomorrow?

Nick knew that something was wrong the moment he entered the room. The tense, pale, slightly nauseous look on Courtney's face was a dead giveaway. He walked up behind her, put his hands on her shoulders, and bent his head so that his mouth was next to her free ear. "What's up?" he whispered.

She covered the mouthpiece with one palm and hissed, "It's Father Castagna!"

He cursed inwardly. Gramma had been busy since he had spoken with her that afternoon. He gestured for her to give him the telephone. "Father? This is Nick."

"Oh, good, I wanted to talk to you, too, and your grandmother didn't know where to reach you."

Nick knew the truth of the matter was that his grandmother hadn't wanted to admit to the priest that he was living with Courtney. Although she was pregnant, living in sin was another issue altogether. Before he could say anything, Father Castagna continued, "As I told your fiancée, we have . . ."

It was out of Nick's hands. He recognized that fact, as surely as he recognized the inevitable passage of time. He and Courtney were going to have their wedding the third Saturday of September at noon in St. Cecelia's in Brooklyn. Their approval of the arrangements was just a formality. Helpless against the combined forces of Anna Trielo and God, he agreed.

By the time Courtney called her parents in Connecticut, she was firmly convinced that she and Nick had made a grave error in not proceeding directly from her office to the nearest Rhode Island magistrate. She considered it nothing short of a miracle that they had managed to commit themselves only to the date, time, and place of the wedding, with all other details to be discussed at Sunday manicotti. As far as she could tell, however, Nick's family had the same definition of "to be discussed" as Mussolini, leaving her with a sneaking suspicion that she was not going to enjoy herself at Sunday's dinner.

Nick sat and watched Courtney dial the telephone, silently praying that she wasn't going to hate him before this circus was over. He should have known better, he chastised himself. He knew precisely what his family had in mind, down to the last cookie. He had been in all four of his sisters' weddings and knew that Italian excess at its most extreme was not a pretty picture. He just knew Courtney was going to hate it.

Unfortunately, he also knew from thirty-four years of practical experience that "to be discussed" was just a euphemism. What was really going to happen was that his entire family was going to badger Court until she agreed to do everything that Gramma Trielo wanted. He wasn't going to be able to do a thing to stop it. The only thing that would accomplish that was an act of God. Something along the line of a tidal wave destroying Brooklyn should do it.

She didn't have the slightest idea what she was in for, he reflected, as he listened to her greet her mother in a calm, collected voice. He wondered idly if they could still try for Rhode Island between now and Sunday.

Her parents were taking this quite well, all things considered, Courtney thought. It wasn't every day they learned that their only daughter, now seven months pregnant with their first grandchild, was finally going to marry the father and their son-in-law-to-be was a professional tag-team wrestler.

"Wrestler," Mrs. Welsch repeated incredulously. Somehow, she'd always had the idea she'd get a doctor or a lawyer in the family. Wrestler?

"That's right, Mother. The Brawny Buccaneers."

"I don't believe I've ever heard of them."

That didn't surprise Courtney; her mother's social circle didn't seem like professional wrestling types. "They're going to be on television tomorrow morning," she offered. "Nick's the one with the dark hair. His partner Steve is the blond."

There was silence on the other end of the line, and Courtney wondered if they'd been disconnected. Finally, her mother hesitantly asked, "Courtney, dear . . . this professional wrestling business . . . is there any money in it?"

"Apparently. He makes more money than I do."

"Oh."

"He went to Cornell. And graduated," she added as an afterthought.

"Oh."

Courtney's mother fell silent again, and she could almost hear her thinking. She had no doubt that her mother was considering that Nick was, at least, prepared to pursue an alternate career somewhere down the road. She had considered the likelihood of that herself, although she hadn't wanted to say anything to Nick about it. Things were still a little touchy at the moment.

"Courtney, I was thinking . . ." Mrs. Welsch began. Her voice sounded more optimistic than it had, so she must have reached the same conclusion that Courtney had. "If you'd like, maybe we could plan a reception up here for you, say at Christmas. If we pick a date in the next few weeks, we can even include it on the announcements. You haven't ordered them yet, have you?"

"That'd be nice, Mother." It would be. She knew the kind of sedate, elegant parties that her mother planned. She took a deep breath and braced herself for the worst. "I believe that Nick's family is planning a reception for us, too."

"We'll have to make certain that they don't conflict. Have they settled on a date yet?"

"The third Saturday in September," Courtney answered reluctantly. "Right after the wedding."

"Courtney, I don't understand. Exactly why are you waiting until next month to get married?"

Courtney opened her mouth and then closed it again. Finally, she forced herself to say the words that were going to break her mother's heart. "Nick's family is planning on a real wedding. Think lavish beyond your wildest imagination. And then multiply that times five."

There was a profound silence on the other end of the line, and then Courtney's mother gasped in horror. Obviously, she'd gotten a fairly accurate picture of the wedding that the Trielos had in mind.

*   *   *

Saturday passed in blissful peace, only because Nick planned it that way and then executed his plan with a single-minded efficiency that would have done Maggie proud. They stayed in the sanctuary of her apartment, secure in the knowledge that the ever-faithful and highly-paid doorman wouldn't permit unannounced guests, including reporters and Trielos, to intrude upon them. Taking the telephone off the hook served to deny electronic access to those two unwelcome species.

Nick pampered Courtney endlessly, making amends for Sunday's ordeal in advance of the fact. After settling her on the sofa in front of Bugs Bunny cartoons, he made pecan waffles, from scratch, for breakfast. She spent the afternoon curled up with a trashy novel and freshly-squeezed lemonade. Dinner was delivered, at obscene expense, from one of the finest restaurants in the city and was accompanied by candlelight and a bottle of non-alcoholic champagne. Afterward, he ran her a bubble bath, which they shared, and then gave her a wonderfully relaxing massage.

At the time, Courtney was thrilled and overwhelmed by the hedonistic pleasure of being pampered and cosseted in such a royal manner. The following day, however, she would have said that nothing on earth could compensate for what she was forced to endure at the hands of Nick's family.

The entire Trielo tribe congregated in Gramma Trielo's two-bedroom, third-story walkup was a formidable sight that immediately explained most of the demands they had made on Friday. It was no wonder that her suggestion of a hundred or so wedding guests had been met with such horror; the immediate Trielo family was comprised of seventy-five people. Their determination for a guest list of a thousand began to make sense. So did the fact that they were more upset about her refusal to marry Nick than they were about her pregnancy; with a third of the women of childbearing age pregnant and another third nursing, it was apparent that supplementing the numbers at such gatherings was their primary purpose in life.

Courtney, as the woman half responsible for the latest contribution to the effort, was greeted with open arms and food. Gramma Trielo, convinced that Courtney was malnourished, urged cookies on her the moment she and Nick entered the apartment, and neither Courtney's assertion that she could wait for dinner, nor Nick's insistence that he was trying to restrict her sugar intake, could dissuade her.

"But, Nicky, she's too thin!" Gramma argued vehemently. "Look at her . . . nothing but skin and bones!"

"And stomach," he muttered under his breath.

Gramma Trielo didn't hear him, but Courtney did, and she glared at him meaningfully.

"She needs it," Gramma continued, undeterred. "Your Courtney's due the same time as Carmella, and . . ."

Nick glanced across the room at the cousin in question who, he had heard one of his sisters say, had gained sixty-two pounds since the beginning of her pregnancy. He repressed the urge to make the obvious comment, which he knew was unkind. With carefully-enforced diplomacy, he said, "Gramma, the doctor says Court's fine."

"Pah! What do doctors know? I gained . . ."

Nick knew that silence was the response of choice. He had seen photographs of Gramma Trielo when she was first married, when she'd weighed something in the neighborhood of a hundred pounds. Now, a good push would send the round little woman rolling all the way to Queens.

The inquisition didn't end with questions about Courtney's pregnancy. Nick had known it wouldn't. Within minutes, all four of his sisters descended, armed with dog-eared back issues of *Bride's* magazine and *Modern Bride*.

"Courtney, do you like green?" Lisa asked. "We all look good in green."

"Yellow's not very good for us," Gina chimed in.

"Or maybe raspberry," Toni offered. "It's like pink, except brighter."

Nick squeezed her shoulder sympathetically as her wide eyes moved from face to face with each new suggestion. She looked as if she wanted to flee immediately, forgetting about both the cannoli and the wedding.

"We have to decide quickly," Marie added frantically. "There's only four weeks to get the dresses made before the wedding . . ."

"Why don't you take them home and look at them?" Gina told her. "We each went through and put our initials on the dresses we liked. Nick can give you my number and you can call me in a day or two and then we'll go see Mrs. Marino."

"She's wonderful," Toni said. "She can make any dress, just from looking at the pictures. And she can make your dress, too . . ."

"She's very good. She made Marcie's dress." Lisa' voice lowered confidentially. "She was expecting, too but Mrs. Marino did such a good job, you could hardl tell. . . ."

Courtney considered the size of her stomach. It woul take a magician to conceal it so well that "you coul hardly tell."

"Would the four of you back off?" Nick sighed, exas perated. His sisters were meeting his worst expectation with a vengeance.

"But, Nick . . ." Gina protested.

"Court'll look them over and get back to you," he sai firmly. "Right now, she's got more important things on he mind than what you're going to wear for the wedding."

"Caterers?"

Nick gave serious consideration to doing bodily har to his sisters. He wondered yet another time if it were to late for them to elope. He missed most of what came nex hearing only chicken and ziti.

"What's ziti?" Courtney whispered, so quietly that on

he could hear her. It was the first thing she had said since the interrogation began.

"Pasta," he explained. "Somewhere between rigatoni and manicotti."

The last part of the explanation didn't really help. "I was . . . sort of . . . thinking of . . . hot and cold hors d'oeuvres," she suggested tentatively.

"No meal?" the four sisters chorused in collective horror.

"You can't have a wedding without feeding people!" Nick's mother protested.

Courtney conjured up a mental picture of Julie and Taylor's reception, which had been a cocktail party with precisely that menu. There had been mountains of food, although none of it had been served on plates bigger than her hand. "Steamed shrimp and miniature crab quiches aren't feeding people?"

"But you have to have a real meal!" Lisa insisted.

"It isn't a wedding without a real meal!" Gramma Trielo rejoined the argument. "Who's saying they don't want a meal?"

TWELVE

The Trielos wanted the parameters of the guest list t[o]
encompass the entire Italian population of Brooklyn.

Courtney wanted to exclude anyone outside their imme[-]
diate families, Julie and Taylor, Khalid and Selena, an[d]
Steve.

The Trielo sisters, as a collective unit, wanted her t[o]
wear a real bridal gown and veil. They wanted to be i[n]
the bridal party, complete with bridesmaids' gowns, hat[s,]
gloves, flowers, and dyed-to-match shoes. They wante[d]
their daughters, in descending order of age, to be juni[or]
bridesmaids, flower girls, and a miniature bride.

Courtney wanted to wear a discreet dress that conceale[d]
as much of her stomach as possible. She wanted Julie, i[n]
her green garden-party dress, as her only attendant. Sh[e]
wanted to know what, in heaven's name, a miniature bri[de]
was, but didn't have the guts to ask.

The Trielos wanted to know where she intended to fi[nd]
out bridal registries, what china and crystal patterns sh[e]
wanted, and what color scheme she had in each of th[e]
rooms in her apartment. They wanted to make dates f[or]
showers, gown fittings, and cookie-baking parties. The[y]
wanted to recommend halls, caterers, and bands for th[e]

172

reception, bakers for the wedding cake, and honeymoon locations.

Courtney wanted to tell them that she had all the china and crystal and sheets and towels that she needed. She wanted to ask why they were going to get a caterer and a baker and then still bake themselves. She wanted to know what right-thinking human being would suggest a tropical beach vacation to a woman who would be in her ninth month of pregnancy.

What the Trielos really wanted was a spectacular wedding to end all spectacular weddings, something along the line of the royal wedding of Charles and Diana.

What Courtney really wanted was to be left alone.

Throughout the long cab ride back to Manhattan from Brooklyn, Nick kept Courtney cradled against his side, one of his arms draped comfortingly around her. He couldn't tell whether or not it helped her, but he felt better just making the effort. That she hadn't said a word since their escape made him extremely uneasy. He wasn't sure whether her grim silence was engendered by hurt feelings, anger, worry, or exhaustion. It didn't matter; regardless of the cause, he felt responsible for it.

Nick had known that the afternoon would be neither easy nor pleasant for Courtney; his relatives, however, had proved to be even more difficult and unpleasant than he had thought was possible, descending upon her with all the Italian determination that had carried Caesar's troops as far as Britain. He wouldn't blame her if she were absolutely furious with them and him. He should have done something to shield her from their damned persistence. She'd be justified if she hit him with another piece of crystal as soon as they got back to the apartment.

Unconsciously, he began to stroke her upper arm, and her head nuzzled against his shoulder as she emitted a low sigh and closed her eyes.

Maybe, if he were lucky, she wasn't angry, just tired.

She should have known that Friday's telephone calls were, like tremors before an earthquake, omens of worse to come. As she leaned into the comforting bulk of Nick, Courtney told herself that she should have paid more attention to what they had been trying to tell her. If she had, Sunday afternoon with the Trielos wouldn't have come as the utter shock it had been. She had felt so overwhelmed by everything. There were so many of them, all coming at her at once, every last one of them filled with unshakable opinions about their wedding.

She absolutely, positively, wanted no part of white wedding dresses and veils, fleets of bridesmaids, and pasta and sauce for a thousand. It was both ludicrous and tacky in the extreme. Her parents would be horrified. She gave a deep sigh that threatened to turn into tears and shuddered

Nick noticed it at once, and wondered with chagrin which part of the afternoon she was recalling. "Court I'm so sorry. I never meant for them to come at you like a pack of steamrollers, but once they started, there was no stopping them."

"I know, Nick. Can we?"

"Stop them? I doubt it."

As awful as Sunday afternoon had been, Courtney just knew that Monday morning was going to be infinitely worse. There was still that flock of reporters camped outside the apartment building, all of whom would undoubtedly migrate to her office during the day. And then there were her bosses. Lord only knew what they would say about the unsavory, unwanted attention she had suddenly brought to the firm.

She managed to get past the reporters; her bosses were another story. When the elevator doors opened, a delegation of four gray-suited senior partners was waiting in the lobby. She told herself that it could have been worse; they could have dragged in the junior partners, and she would have had to face ten of them instead of only four. Four of them was more than sufficient.

Not even allowing her the opportunity to leave her brief-case in her office, they swept her away to the conference room. It wasn't a good sign. The last time the conference room had been used was for a four-on-one confrontation, when they'd fired Scott Preston for unethical conduct.

The heavy door shut behind them, isolated within the room's oppressive oak-panelled confines, the four senior partners, Peter, Franklin, and Charles McGuinn, and Jason Becker, took seats around the huge table. At the invitation of Franklin McGuinn, the eldest of the brothers, Courtney lowered herself in a chair, trying not to appear as clumsy and unwieldy as she felt.

"Well, Courtney," Franklin McGuinn began. "You've been with us for eight years, and you've always been an asset to us. We've been pleased with the conscientiousness and thoroughness of your work, your clients are all very happy with you, and recently we've been getting a great many referrals asking for you."

But . . . Courtney added mentally. She knew they hadn't called her here to compliment her work; if she hadn't learned anything else in the eight years she'd been with them, she'd learned what was and wasn't like them.

"The last several weeks have been something of a trial for all of us," Charles McGuinn interjected. "Generally, we try to avoid publicity as much as possible. Recently, however, it seems as if we've attracted a great deal of media attention, first with that insider information case and then . . ."

"Courtney," Peter McGuinn filled the gap left by Charles McGuinn's fading voice, "about the article in Fri-day's newspaper. It came as a bit of a shock to all of us when we found out . . ."

Here it comes, Courtney told herself silently. Friday's newspaper. She gulped and prepared herself for the worst.

"Why didn't you tell anyone that Nick Trielo was the

father of your baby?'' Jason Becker interrupted with his usual bluntness.

"I . . . I . . ." Courtney attempted. She couldn't seem to get any further than that.

"He's a wrestler, Courtney," Becker continued. "In today's market, a celebrity. Did you really believe that no one would find out?"

"I . . ."

"Back off, Jason." Franklin McGuinn gave him a piercing stare. His eyes and voice were softer when he turned his attention back to Courtney. "We can't help it, Courtney. We're concerned about the way the firm looks. Maybe in the world of celebrities, things like this are common, but in business, the appearance of respectability means everything."

She had known it would happen. They were letting her down easy, but were firing her nonetheless. Maybe she could get into a less conservative field, like publishing or advertising.

"We realize that, legally, we have no right to ask you about your personal life," Franklin McGuinn continued, "but . . . Courtney . . . is there any possibility of you and Mr. Trielo marrying . . ." He glanced uneasily at her stomach. ". . . soon?"

"Julie?" Courtney asked, as soon as the telephone stopped ringing.

"Court, is that you? Where have you been all weekend? I've been trying and trying to call you, but there hasn't been any answer . . ." Julie was tearing on at a breakneck pace that was only going to be stopped by brutal interruption.

"We unplugged the phone after Friday night."

"I should have known! I'm sorry about the article, Court. How'd they find out?"

"Nick thinks that there was a reporter eavesdropping in

the restaurant where he met Khalid for lunch the other day."

"Lord, what a mess," Julie groaned. "How are they taking it there at work?"

"Better than I expected," Courtney told her. "They didn't fire me, and it sounds as if I'm still in the running for the junior partnership."

"That's great, Court! I told you what really mattered was how good you were at your job."

Courtney saw no valid reason to disillusion her friend with the gruesome reality that her announcement that she and Nick had set a wedding date had been the only thing that had saved her neck.

"Have you talked to your parents yet?"

"On Friday. They're coming into the city for the wedding. They're not thrilled, but they're coming."

"Wedding?" Julie's voice rose in an excited squeal. "When? I'll be your bridesmaid, of course. What do you think about that voile dress of mine . . . the one that looks like I'm going to a garden party?"

"I'd love it, but it doesn't look as if I'm going to be the only one with any say in the matter."

"What does that mean?"

"How do you feel about parasols and picture hats?"

"Steve?"

"Nick, where have you been all weekend? Khalid and I have been out of our minds . . ."

"Phone's been unplugged. We've been hiding from reporters and relatives."

"Successfully?"

"More or less."

"How's Court taking it?"

"As well as can be expected. Gramma's on the warpath."

"Trying to get you two married off?" In the fifteen years he had known Nick, he had had repeated experience, both first- and second-hand, in dealing with Anna Trielo's iron will.

"Succeeding. What are you doing the third Saturday in September?"

"Being your best man." Steve laughed. "Why are you waiting so long? I would have thought you'd marry Court tomorrow, now that she doesn't have a reason to say no anymore."

"I would, but they have to read the banns for three Sundays, and anyway, it's the first time the church is open . . ."

"Church?" Steve echoed.

"Gramma wants . . ."

". . . orange blossoms and a white dress and . . . Oh, God."

"What's wrong?"

"I just got a mental picture of Court in another month in a wedding gown."

"Probably the same one she sees every time she closes her eyes and shudders."

That evening, as Nick massaged her calves and played "Introduction to Nuclear Physics" tapes to the baby, Courtney told him about her first day out in public since the article disclosing their relationship had appeared in the newspaper. In short, it had been the longest day of her life, even worse than the day the market crashed.

After her royal audience, she had returned to her office, where Maggie was trying to answer the telephone and prepare Courtney's deposition simultaneously. It was more than one human could handle. Finally, she'd admitted defeat and requisitioned someone from the steno pool to answer the phone and run interference so that they could get some work done. The ploy succeeded only until the harried girl informed the Assistant District Attorney that Ms. Welsch had no comment at this time.

He had not been amused and called Jason Becker to demand an explanation for the runaround he was getting from a subpoenaed witness in a federal investigation. Becker's face was purple as he relayed the message that Courtney could consider herself in contempt if she didn't return his call immediately, if not sooner. Courtney apologized profusely and promised to do just that as soon as she got back to her own office.

The task was delayed only slightly by the presence of a new girl from the steno pool at Maggie's station. In Courtney's absence, Maggie had called the first girl a dimwit and threatened her with severe bodily harm, precipitating her immediate resignation and departure, as well as some ugly muttering about abusiveness and the Labor Relations Board. While Maggie went and tried to make peace with the head of the steno pool and the office manager, Courtney called the Assistant District Attorney's office and groveled.

The first group of secretaries to go to lunch came back with reports of a sizable contingency of reporters and photographers waiting outside for Courtney, who then called the deli down the block and offered the moon if they would deliver. The delivery boy, an unemployed actor, subsequently traded Courtney's lunch to an enterprising reporter for the private telephone number of the producer of a top-rated soap opera. With Courtney's corned-beef-and-Swiss on rye as a hostage, the reporter got as far as Maggie's desk, where Maggie liberated it before handing the man over to security. As the elevator door closed behind them, everyone in the office heard him threaten to sue the firm for battery.

In the afternoon, the mob outside tripled in size as a result of two unrelated but equally cataclysmic events. The first was the Assistant District Attorney's news conference, at which he announced the discovery of the location of Courtney's client's secret bank accounts, a disclosure which sent every reporter at the conference scurrying over to Courtney's building for some comment from her. The second was a casual remark by one of the photographers that Courtney's eyes were purple, "just like Elizabeth Taylor's," an innocent enough observation until the grapevine got hold of it and people flocked from all over the city in response to unsubstantiated rumors that Elizabeth Taylor was in the building.

Maggie had been frantic about how she was going to spirit Courtney out of the building and past the reporters this time; she had already checked out the route she had used on Friday and it was under media surveillance. As it turned out, the matter was handled by the lawyers on the fifteenth floor after one of their associates, coincidentally a very pregnant brunette, tried to leave the building. The reporters and photographers, on the alert for a pregnant brunette, mobbed the woman, who fled back into the building in near-hysteria, prompting her bosses' insistence that security barricade a path through the throng to the street. It had been a relatively simple matter for Courtney and Maggie to run the gauntlet to a waiting cab.

Nick listened sympathetically to Courtney's recital of the day's events and gave her a back and neck massage, too, during which she drifted off to sleep. He was relieved, because he hadn't known how to tell her that the riot on Wall Street had been the third story on "Live at Five" that afternoon. He still didn't know how to tell her that his grandmother had made an appointment with the seamstress for the following day.

"Another month, you say?" Mrs. Marino asked, her pin-filled mouth twisting thoughtfully as she examined the tape measure around Courtney's stomach.

"Third Saturday in September," Courtney forced out with as much civility as she could muster. After all, Mrs. Marino wasn't the instigator of this farce, only responsible for its execution. The real guilty parties were the four Trielo sisters, their mother, and Gramma Trielo, who sat on the far side of the sewing room, alternately watching the proceedings and perusing bridal magazines.

"Anna, what do you think?" Mrs. Marino turned to the woman for advice. "Another three inches?"

"Add four. My Nicky's son's going to be a big baby."

Silently, Courtney appealed to Julie, who was standing by helplessly awaiting her own fitting.

"Mom, how much longer are we going to be here?" Lisa's daughter, Christi, ten, whined. "I've got softball practice."

"Shh, just wait," her mother hissed. "How many times are you going to be in your Uncle Nicky's wedding?"

One, God willing, Courtney answered mentally. And that was one too many.

Christi wasn't the most annoying of the crew, although she hadn't stopped grousing since their arrival in Mrs. Marino's sewing room. The grandmother of the groom had suddenly assumed all the rights and privileges normally reserved for the Queen Mother. The bridesmaids had yet to agree on the colors or styles of their gowns and accessories. The junior bridesmaids all wanted to be somewhere else. The flower girls were bored and cranky and needed naps. And the miniature bride, just shy of three, had wet herself twice.

If it weren't for Julie, Courtney would have screamed like a madwoman. Only Julie remained sane through it all, a stalwart but thoroughly ineffective source of support and comfort.

"No, no, no," Anna insisted. "Rosa, you've got to move the waist higher so she doesn't show."

Courtney met Julie's eyes again. Silently, each communicated the understanding that Courtney's stomach was going to show, even if they moved the waist all the way up to her forehead. It was funny, but both of them bit back laughter that they knew would only irritate Nick's grandmother.

Mrs. Marino draped the fabric from a point farther up Courtney's torso. "Maybe a ruffle . . ."

"No," Courtney said firmly. "No ruffle. I agreed to

lace, but absolutely no ruffle.'' She was cooperating with this lunacy, but she had her limits.

"But, Courtney . . .'' Anna began.

"No. I'll look like a barrel if you put a ruffle over my stomach!'' She might be pregnant, but that didn't mean that the last traces of her vanity had fled.

"My sister's girl used a ruffle to hide . . .''

"Gramma, she was only five months pregnant,'' Gina interjected. As far as Courtney was concerned, it was the first thing any of the Trielo sisters had said that day that made sense. "Courtney's right. She's too big. A ruffle wouldn't do anything except make her look bigger.''

"Can we have gloves?'' Toni asked. "This pair seems to be the same color as the dress.''

"They are!'' Marie agreed. "That way we can have cap sleeves on the gowns. Even though the wedding's in September, it's liable to be warm.''

Indignant, Courtney fumed that the heat of September hadn't occurred to anyone when they picked long puffed sleeves for her dress. After all, she was the one most likely to keel over from the heat.

"Julie, I'm sorry,'' Courtney apologized in the cab on their way back to Manhattan. "I'd never have asked you to be in the wedding if I'd known that they were going to go so far overboard. I'll give you part of the money for it. How about I buy the accessories?''

"Court, that's okay,'' Julie lied. The accessories alone came to nearly two hundred dollars. "We have the money.''

"That's not the point. You expected to wear something you already had.''

"Not after you told me that Nick's family was running this show.'' She had come prepared to agree to anything, no matter how outrageous. When the Trielo sisters had settled on hot-pink floral dresses that made them look like extras from *Gone With The Wind*, complete with crinolines, picture hats, and parasols, Julie had bit her lip and nodded, in spite of Courtney's quiet but unmistakable sound of disgust.

"We should have drawn the line at the shoes." Nick's sisters had insisted that they have dyed-to-match shoes, in spite of the fact that Courtney had argued that no one had any earthly use for hot-pink shoes beyond the wedding.

"If it makes them happy and keeps peace, I'm willing to go for the extra fifty."

"Nick's going to be furious."

He was. "The dresses and stuff came to how much?" he roared. "And you and Julie agreed to it?"

"We didn't have much choice," Courtney sighed. "Between your grandmother and your mother and your sisters . . ."

"Give me the phone," he snapped, reaching for it.

"Now, Nick . . ."

"I'm serious. They can't do this to you and Julie. If they want to assume the national debt, that's one thing, but . . ."

"Nick, they already did. It's too late."

When he and Steve went for tuxedo fittings, it became apparent to Nick how Courtney and Julie had been so thoroughly overcome and overruled. Quite plainly, they had been both outtalked and outnumbered. Nick and Steve, in spite of prior warning, were only marginally better off than the women had been. Not only did they have to contend with Gramma and Mama Trielo and Nick's four sisters, but Nick's brothers-in-law and nephews were also there, obviously briefed in advance to cooperate with the Trielo women's plans. It had been less of a challenge when Nick and Steve had faced the Killer Hillbillies.

"This color goes best with the girls' dresses," Anna insisted, waving a swatch of fabric that fully met Nick's most ghastly expectations in front of a sky-blue tuxedo. With the unwelcome discovery that the pinks clashed, she had resorted to a subordinate floral color.

Nick looked to Steve for support before he began hesitantly, "Gramma, can we consider black or gray, maybe?" He couldn't, in all good conscience, inflict that color on his worst enemy, let alone his best friend. To say nothing of himself.

"With bright pink ruffled shirts and roses on the lapels, it'll be perfect," she continued, undaunted by his lack of enthusiasm.

"Nick, all your sisters . . ." his mother began.

"We had colored tuxedos at my wedding, remember?" Lisa asked.

Nick remembered. He had been forced to wear an orange tuxedo. He had felt like a tall pumpkin.

"We had colored tuxedos, too," Gina added.

That had been the lavender, Nick recalled.

"And at our wedding," Marie contributed.

Mint green.

"And ours," Toni offered.

That had been the worst. Yellow. Bright. Banana yellow.

"If you won't go for black or gray, how about white?" Nick suggested. "Or cream?"

"But, Nick!" all four of his sisters chorused.

"Steve?" he appealed.

"I have a black tuxedo," Steve offered. "It fits and everything. If you let me wear it, I'll wear any color shirt, tie, and cummerbund you want."

"I have a black tuxedo, too," Nick said. They had bought them for Khalid's wedding, when they had discovered, to no one's real surprise, that none of the rental agencies in the city could successfully fit all of the men in the bridal party.

"I don't like it," Anna insisted, a determined expression on her face.

"Neither do I," Nick's mother grumbled.

"Look, Gramma, Mama, I really don't see any point in renting a tuxedo that's not going to fit, when I have one that does. And so does Steve."

It was the one argument they couldn't refute. Years of Christmas and birthday shopping for Nick had taught them that finding clothing to fit him was at least a challenge and a sure route to madness at its most extreme.

"Frankie," Nick tried, appealing to the tailor, who had reconstructed his clothes on more than one occasion. "What are your chances of locating two size fifties in that color? In three weeks?"

Frankie shook his head reluctantly and admitted, "Slim to none." He didn't like losing the business, but there was no point in promising them something he couldn't deliver. Besides, he was essentially a traditionalist, and his sympathies were with Nick and the black tuxedo.

Three generations of Trielo women looked belligerent, but they didn't say anything.

"That settles that, then. Black tuxedos for everyone. Pick the shirts and things that you want, and we'll take them."

In the cab en route to Manhattan, Steve opened the bag, peeked at the contents inside, and shuddered visibly yet another time. "I did something wrong in a past life and this is God's vengeance."

"Don't gripe," Nick told him, although he wanted to growl himself. The sky-blue accessories his grandmother had selected for him weren't an improvement on Steve's flamingo pink. "You got off easier than Julie. This is costing her a bundle that I keep wanting to apologize for."

"Nick, I'm sorry, but you couldn't have made me pay what they were asking for that blue thing, let alone put it on my body."

"If our bodies weren't so big, you wouldn't have had a choice in the matter."

"I haven't been so grateful for my size since that jerk in Chicago accused me of trying to pick up his girl."

"You were trying to pick up his girl. And if you hadn't outweighed him by fifty pounds, he would have taken you apart limb by limb."

"Didn't get the girl, though." Steve shrugged with only minor regret. "She got mad when I hit him."

"Serves you right." Nick thought about it and grinned. "Maybe that's what you did to deserve that shirt and tie."

"Court's really gonna hate this."

She did. "Oh, Nick, they're positively ghastly," Courtney choked when Nick and Steve showed her their new shirts, ties, and cummerbunds. "How could you let them do this to you?"

"This, from the woman who went for bridal fittings with them last week?"

"Never mind. I know how they did it."

"At least we held out for black tuxedos," Steve offered.

"Only because they couldn't get them in periwinkle."

"Sky blue," Nick corrected.

"Whatever."

By the time Nick returned from showing Steve out of the apartment, Courtney was sound asleep on the sofa. He stood and watched her sleep, knowing he wouldn't disturb her; he hadn't the day before when he'd actually put together an entire baby swing in the living room, cursing as he did because none of the six languages in which the instructions were printed was English. As he thought about it, he realized she'd done the same thing the day before that. . . . In fact, every single afternoon for the last two weeks or so. Each time, she'd slept until he'd finally awakened her for dinner. Although he knew that it was perfectly normal for pregnant women to take naps, he didn't really think that it was normal for them to continue sleeping until someone woke them up.

It worried him. All she did was sleep, and it didn't appear to do her a bit of good. There were dark purple shadows under her eyes and she always looked as exhausted as if she hadn't slept in weeks. And her stomach kept getting bigger and bigger while the rest of her was just skin and bones, as if the baby were sapping all the strength from her body. He brushed several dark wisps of hair away from her face and it occurred to him that her delicacy was beginning to look like fragility, and his worry evolved into out-and-out terror.

Panic-stricken, Nick dragged the telephone into the bedroom and called Selena, who confirmed what he suspected, that Courtney's behavior wasn't entirely normal. His next call was to her doctor's office. Her response to his questions infuriated him. As he hung up the phone, he cursed himself for being in Philadelphia and missing Courtney's last appointment. He also cursed Courtney for not telling him everything that the doctor had said. His third call was to Jason Becker.

THIRTEEN

Nick restrained himself until after Courtney had consumed a good, nutritious meal containing all of the four basic food groups. At that time, he baldly announced, "Jason Becker's agreed to give you a leave of absence until Thanksgiving."

Courtney stared at him incredulously, as if he were speaking another language. The color drained from her face. Finally she choked out, "What?"

"You are officially on leave of absence until Thanksgiving," Nick repeated firmly.

"Since when?"

"Since tonight. I talked to your doctor this afternoon and it seems that there were a few things you forgot to mention after your last visit." He sounded every bit as cold and unyielding as he had the day he had moved into her apartment. "I called her because I couldn't figure out why you were sleeping so much and she told me that there wasn't a damn thing wrong with you except stress and exhaustion. She also told me that she had told you last week that you were going to have to take it easy."

The color rushed back into Courtney's face and she glared at him angrily.

"Easy," he continued tightly, "is not generally defined as cutting back to forty hours."

"My job," Courtney finally managed to force out, "is very demanding. I can't just take off for three months!"

"Your pregnancy," Nick countered, "is very demanding, too. And you can take three months. I already fixed it."

Courtney went white all over again. "Fixed it?"

"I called Jason Becker after I spoke with your doctor."

"You called Jason Becker?" She was livid. He reminded himself that he had known she would be.

"Yes. Is there any particular reason you neglected to mention that you're allowed thirteen weeks of maternity leave?"

Courtney opened her mouth and closed it again several times, but no sound emerged except a strangled squeak.

"What is your basic problem, Courtney?" Nick's voice cracked with both anger and concern. "Are you afraid they'll find out the world still rotates without you?"

Again, she tried to speak and failed, giving Nick the opportunity to continue his tirade.

"Were you going to keep it up until you popped out the baby under your desk and then go right back to work like some slave in a cotton field?"

She winced, but he plowed on mercilessly.

"Don't you give a damn about the baby? About yourself? About me?"

Nick stopped then. He couldn't go on, not once Courtney began crying. He felt like a monster when she did because she didn't howl or gush dramatically like his sisters when she cried; instead, she whimpered like a hurt kitten as huge individual tears trailed down her cheeks.

"Oh, God, Court," he groaned, scooping her up in his arms and carrying her to the sofa. He sat with her on his lap and rubbed her back and arms as he apologized over and over again.

Gradually, she calmed, and he lowered his head to nuzzle the soft skin on the back of her neck. "Are you okay, hon?"

"I feel lousy, Nick," she sniffed, her violet eyes filling with tears. "My back hurts and my ankles are swollen . . ."

"Shh," he consoled her softly, turning on the sofa so that he cradled her against his chest. "It won't be for much longer now."

"Six weeks! I can't take six more weeks of this!"

He didn't protest her statement, although the doctor had told them both that the baby was so big that she didn't think Courtney could carry for six more weeks.

Nick's hand moved to stroke the taut surface of her stomach and, involuntarily and irrationally, he became aroused. Wincing, he hoped she didn't notice. During their last visit, the doctor had forbidden sex until after the baby was born, and he knew that it would upset her even further if she were aware of how abstinence was affecting him.

Her head shot forward away from his chest as she felt the pressure of his erection against her backside. "Oh, hell, Nick, this is ridiculous!" she wailed.

He eased his hips away from her, cursing his traitorous body silently.

She pulled away from him and slumped, hanging her head over the back of the sofa. Sighing, she whispered, "Nick maybe we should wait until after the baby's born . . ."

He leaned forward to put his arms around her again and rested his chin on the top of her head, inhaling the sweet smell of her hair. "I know that, honey. I can wait. The doctor said . . ."

She shook her head, knowing he had misunderstood her. "That goes without saying, Nick. I mean that we should wait . . ."

A chill started in Nick's stomach. Hesitantly, he prompted, "Wait for what?"

"To get married."

The icy terror radiated throughout his veins, violentl

quelling his arousal. He didn't think he wanted to hear anything else she was going to say.

Courtney took a deep breath and continued. "If we wait until afterward, we can have a big blow-out wedding just like they all want . . ."

"We're having a big wedding now," he tried to reason with her.

"Which, at this stage of the game, is just ridiculous."

"Because of the baby? Court, what are people going to do—chase you down the aisle and stone us?"

"Isn't a white dress and veil over this stomach the least little bit ludicrous?"

"False advertising? Court, if only virgins were entitled to wear white dresses, the bridal gown industry would have gone bankrupt years ago."

She cast him another baleful look that spoke volumes without words.

"Honey, I wish you wouldn't worry about what people think . . ."

"Nick," she snapped. "Did it ever occur to you that I might be concerned about something else besides what people might think?"

"What's wrong?" He was genuinely puzzled by the sharp left turn their argument was taking.

"What's wrong?" she echoed, her voice rising with potential hysteria.

He suspected that he was missing something vital, something that had been making Courtney anxious ever since the wedding plans had been set into motion, something that had nothing whatsoever to do with her continuing distaste for his career, her sudden, unwelcome loss of her privacy, or even his family's propensity for bad taste. Quietly, he tried again, "Honey, please tell me . . ."

She turned her head, burying her face in his chest. He felt silent tears dampening the front of his shirt.

"Court?"

She raised her face to his, her bottom lip jutting out

and trembling. "I . . . always wanted to be a . . . pretty bride . . ."

Nick's brow furrowed. "Pretty?"

She nodded, her expression even more miserable. "Pretty," she repeated adamantly. "Nick, every little girl always wants to be pretty for her wedding."

He cupped her warm, wet cheeks with his hands. "Court, you're beautiful."

"I'm fat."

"You're not fat; you're pregnant."

"Same difference. I don't have a waist either way."

"Oh, honey . . ." His arms encircled her tightly, holding her to him. "It doesn't matter . . ."

"To me it does." She shuddered in his arms.

"Court, I love you. You love me. What difference . . ."

She pulled away from him. "Nick, I look like a cow!"

"No, Courtney!" Nick's fingers clenched around a fistful of Courtney's hair, pulling it so roughly that he jerked her head back. Neither one of them noticed, however, because the pain within each of them vastly overwhelmed it. "It was bad enough before, when I was an embarrassment to you, but I'll be damned if I'll let you do this to us!"

"I want to be pretty for you, Nick!" she wailed.

"Court, I think you're beautiful, dammit!" he bellowed. "I love you and I'm going to marry you the third Saturday in September if it's the last thing I do! And I don't want to hear any more of this nonsense about postponing the wedding!"

She was going to make another excuse. Nick knew it even before she opened her mouth to speak. And he wasn't going to allow it, not again, because the first thing he knew, she'd have herself convinced, again, that she shouldn't marry him. He tightened his grasp on her hair and gripped her jaw with his free hand, holding her head still as his lips found hers with an urgency born of desperation.

Surprised by his sudden ardor, Courtney gasped, allowing him access to the depths of her mouth. His tongue thrust inside, exploring the tender tissue of her inner lips, the serrated edges of her teeth, the sinuous grace of her tongue, in a way he hadn't dared to risk since the doctor had told them they couldn't make love. He knew that it would tie him up in knots, get him all hot and bothered with no hope of release, but he could only hope that it would have the same effect on her. He had to remind her that they belonged together, in spite of the qualms she had about the differences in their familial and cultural heritages, their careers and goals . . .

As she began to return his kiss, Nick loosened his hold on her scalp and jaw, permitting his hands to wander downward to the soft fullness of her breasts. He smiled with satisfaction as his thumbs brushed her nipples and found them already swollen with arousal. He pushed his advantage, knowing that he was going to pay for it whether he stopped now or forged ahead, and told himself that, if necessary, he would sleep standing up under a cold shower.

Courtney arched her back, molding her breast into his palm, begging for more contact. He complied with her silent request and she sighed in response to the sensation. Pressure built inside that had nothing to do with her body's preparations for motherhood.

Nick lowered his head and touched his mouth to the curve of her breast before he realized what he was doing. She shifted in his arms and her nipple slipped across his wet bottom lip and into his mouth. Reflexively, he began to suckle, until a sharp jab against his arousal reminded him that, for now, anyway, Courtney's breasts were full for someone else's gratification. Shuddering as he tried to regain control over his libido, Nick sat up abruptly, towing Courtney along to sit primly beside him.

She watched as he leaned forward, his elbows on his knees and his face in his hands, drawing one ragged breath after another. At last, his breathing calmed and he raise his head to smile wryly at her. "I guess that pretty muc proves it. If I loved you any more and thought you wer any more beautiful, you'd be calling an ambulance for m right now. As it is, I'm off to the showers."

The following morning, Courtney went to her office t get a few things, particularly the file for the grand jur hearings, which were scheduled for the week after th wedding. Because of the subpoena, it was the one obliga tion that couldn't be assigned to someone else.

It was both a pleasure and a surprise that she got a the way from her apartment to the office without encoun tering a single reporter or photographer. Entering he office, she remarked on that feat to Maggie.

"They're all uptown now," Maggie told her. She wa laughing. "I guess your fifteen minutes of fame is over."

Courtney stared at her secretary, puzzled.

"Don't you watch the news or read the papers?"

Maggie knew better than that; after all, she was the on who kept all of Courtney's magazine subscriptions curren It was just that she hadn't seen a paper or turned on th television since the weekend.

"They've got another target now," Maggie explained handing Courtney the afternoon paper from the previou day. "No offense, Courtney, but this one is better."

Courtney began to skim the article, stopped, sat dow behind her desk, and read it word by word.

Maggie was right. In comparison with this, her relation ship with Nick was totally insignificant, as far as newswo thiness went. In a high-class prostitution raid two night before, the police had interrupted the daughter of a Oscar-winning actor in the middle of entertaining a clien Her client, who happened to be the son of a senator wit a national reputation as an anti-drug activist, had well ove a thousand dollars worth of cocaine in his possession an had tested positive for use. Reportedly, the actor's daugh ter had been handcuffed to the bed, a rumor validated by the extremely kinky attire she exhibited in the photographs. The newspaper closed the article with the observation that both the actor and the senator had posted bail for their children.

Although Courtney felt like a voyeur as she read the article, she couldn't stop until she finished. She read several parts of it more than once. Finally, she looked up and met Maggie's eyes.

"I feel like such a jerk," she confessed.

"You should."

"All that time, I held Nick off because I was afraid of a scandal. Now this," she pointed down at the newspaper, "is a scandal."

"It certainly is."

Courtney sighed and wondered how she could apologize to Nick for everything she had said and done. She wondered if it were even possible to do so. She had hurt him with her insistence on treating him like an embarrassing secret and he had kept loving her unconditionally. The truth of the matter was that Nick wasn't an embarrassment at all. What he was was the man she loved and would love for the rest of her life. And if she hadn't been such an idiot, she would have figured it out months ago.

She closed the newspaper and hoisted herself to her feet. "I have to go home, Maggie. I have a lot of making-up to do."

Maggie hugged her, handed her the file, which she almost forgot, and wished her luck. "You know, if you hadn't come to your senses, I might have decided that a secretary didn't have to worry about scandal and taken him for myself."

Courtney shook her head. "Neither should an investments analyst. Particularly when the scandal is all in her own head."

*　　*　　*

In her eagerness to get back to her apartment and Nick, Courtney badgered the cab driver mercilessly, as if the traffic jam were somehow his fault. Finally, the poor man twisted around in his seat and glared back at her.

"You in labor, lady?"

She smiled at him beatifically, oblivious to the annoyance in his voice. "Not yet."

"In that case, would you just pipe down? I can't make this thing fly, you know."

Courtney apologized and the man turned back in his seat and muttered, "Crazy broad."

Ten seconds later, Courtney reached up and tapped on the partition between them.

"What now, lady?"

"I'll just walk from here. We're almost there and it'll be faster."

"Whatever you say, lady," he answered disinterestedly, pulling the handle on the meter.

After levering herself out of the cab, she thrust the money through the window at him, telling him to keep the change.

He glanced at the bill and smiled for the first time as he thanked her.

She bustled up the street, through the lobby of her apartment building, and into the elevator. As she rode upwards, she tapped her foot impatiently and pressed the button repeatedly, as if it would make the car move faster. Finally, it arrived at her floor and she hurried out of it and down the hall of her apartment. Slamming the door behind her, she yelled for Nick.

As he stepped into the living room from the kitchen, she lunged at him, throwing her arms around his neck.

"What is it, honey? What's wrong?" he demanded, worried.

"I love you so much," she replied, grinning broadly, "and I've been such an idiot. Can you ever forgive me?"

He stared down at her, speechless. He didn't have a

clue as to what she was talking about. The only thing that was clear was that she seemed awfully happy about whatever it was that he was supposed to forgive.

She told him everything and he listened, although he didn't understand it all. It wasn't important because he got the gist of it, which was that Courtney finally believed what he had been telling her all along, that the only scandal in their relationship had been the one she had created in her mind. The rest of the world had more interesting and/or important things to worry about than an investments analyst marrying a professional wrestler.

He didn't say "I told you so." It would have been both cruel and unnecessary. Instead, he took her in his arms and gave her congratulatory kisses until they both needed cold showers.

As days passed, Nick's compunctions about railroading Courtney into the leave of absence began to ebb. The dark circles under her eyes faded, as did the tight expression of exhaustion and stress that had been the result of the day-to-day pressures and responsibilities of her job. With only the grand jury hearings ahead of her, she had time to relax and pamper herself as she hadn't been able to do in years. Even she could see the difference, and she almost began to believe Nick when he told her that she was blooming.

The only fly in the ointment was his family, who was still charging full speed ahead with the wedding arrangements. As far as either of them could tell, they had concluded that Courtney's leave of absence was an effort to place herself completely at their disposal.

Nick hadn't been aware of this misconception at first, or he would have nipped it in the bud. He had been spending a lot of time at the gym, making peace with Jake at the same time that he was working off his sexual frustration. By the time Courtney mentioned the perpetual telephone calls to him, the situation was clearly out of control.

* * *

"Nick?" Courtney asked softly. If he was asleep, she didn't want to wake him; while it was upsetting, it just wasn't that important.

He was hovering on the edge of sleep, but he recognized the note of anxiety in her voice. His eyes still closed, his arms tightened around her and he murmured with a sleepy huskiness, "Yeah, Court?"

"Why do they want to bake cookies?"

"What?" he asked drowsily. Cookies?

"Cookies," she repeated. "Your sisters keep calling me and asking me when I can come and bake cookies."

Nick was wide awake now, both eyes open. His sisters. Cookies for the wedding. He should have known they'd get around to it sooner or later.

"When did they call you, Court?" he demanded. "Who called you?"

"I don't understand why they're hiring a caterer and a baker and then baking cookies. Why do we need cookies, Nick?"

Nick groaned miserably. Before this was all over, he was going to throttle one, or possibly all, of his sisters. He had told them Courtney's leave of absence was because she needed the rest.

"I don't know what earthly good I'd be to them, anyway," Courtney babbled on. "Lord knows I'm not domestic, and I don't even know what half of the things are that she was talking about . . . like tor . . . tor . . ."

"Tortoni," Nick supplied, his teeth clenched. "Who called you, Court, and when?"

"Well . . ." She thought for a moment. "First, Gina called me Monday morning while I was working on the statement for the Federal District Attorney's office. Then, while I was meeting with Mr. Jacobs Monday afternoon, Lisa called because I didn't give an answer to Gina. Tuesday morning, your mother . . ."

"Never mind, Court," he snarled, simultaneously tightening his grip on her. "You don't have to give me the whole line-up. Did everyone call?"

He felt her head move against his shoulder. "More or less."

"Don't worry about it, sweetheart," he assured her. "I'll take care of it. I'll talk to them."

"I don't have to go and bake cookies?"

"You don't have to go and bake cookies."

"Good," she sighed, closing her eyes and nuzzling against him.

He closed his eyes, too, holding her.

"Nick?"

"Hmm?"

"You never did answer my question. . . . Why do they want to bake cookies, anyway?"

"Nick?" Courtney asked sleepily.

His body tensed automatically, but he forced his voice to remain even. "Yes, sweetheart?"

"Your grandmother called me today . . ."

"And?" He cringed, anticipating the worst.

"She wanted to remind me that we still haven't picked a band . . ."

He sighed wearily. "I told her last night that we don't need to pick a band. Kyle Phillips already called and made the offer to play for the wedding, so I told him . . ." He felt Courtney go rigid in his arms. "Hon, what's wrong?"

"Kyle Phillips?" she squeaked. "The lead singer of Feroher?"

"Right. Anyway . . ."

"Kyle Phillips is going to play for our wedding?"

"Right. We were . . ."

"You know Kyle Phillips?"

He covered her mouth with his palm. "As I was saying, we were all in the frat together at Cornell."

She knew he was grinning, even in the dark; she could feel it.

"Wanna guess who has the other three tattoos?"

She groaned. "Kyle Phillips has a tattoo like this?" She jabbed him in the chest with her finger.

"Ouch. Watch the nails. Maybe if you're nice to me, I could convince him to let you see it."

"I'll pass." She paused for a moment, thinking. "Nick, what's the handkerchief dance?"

"An old Italian tradition. Don't worry, I wouldn't make you dance with all my aunts in your condition."

She was silent for a bit. "Your aunts?"

"Nick?" Courtney's voice penetrated the darkness.

He groaned inwardly. What had they done now? "Yes, darling?"

"Your Aunt Lucia called me today."

He sighed heavily and then swore. Lucia was inarguably the most maddening of his close relatives. She and Gramma Trielo had been feuding, on and off, for the last fifty years.

"Nick, she wanted to talk about wedding showers—that's plural, you hear?—and baby showers—also plural."

"As in more than one?"

"That's what the word means. Something about the Trielos and the Crivellis . . ." Courtney's voice trailed off and Nick finished for her.

". . . And the Marcantinos. One shower for each, because they don't speak." He remembered the drill from his sisters' weddings.

"Right. Anyway, she's got it all planned out so that we can have all six showers before the wedding. I tried to explain to her that getting to Brooklyn six times in the next two weeks isn't really feasible, given that it takes over an hour in each direction and . . ."

"She didn't understand?" He did. Courtney was in the bathroom every fifteen minutes 'round the clock now that the baby had shifted to lie on her bladder.

"She didn't hear me. I might as well have been talking to a dial tone."

He knew his aunt and it was an accurate assessment.

"I'm really trying to get along with them, Nick. It's just that . . . Is there any way that we could just have one shower? Even one wedding shower and one baby shower?"

"I don't know, sweetheart. The last time it happened, Truman was president."

Courtney groaned, sounding so weary that Nick couldn't stand it.

"Let me call them tomorrow. I'll see what I can do."

The following morning, even before Nick finished his first cup of coffee, he was forced to deal with the matter. He had already listened to one-sided discussions concerning pasta and mother-of-the-bride dresses, and the cake top sounded as if it were going to be Courtney's undoing.

"Gina, I swear to God, if you put those ugly ceramic figures on my wedding cake, I'll throw the whole damn thing out the nearest window," Courtney snarled as she looked down at the picture in the bridal magazine lying open on the coffee table.

"But, Courtney . . ."

"Gina, I said no. And this time, I mean it."

Courtney's sudden determination to put down her size seven, take a stand, and draw the line came as a complete shock to everyone, including her. In an effort to avoid a confrontation, she had agreed to each and every one of their suggestions, no matter how outrageous or ostentatious or tacky, as had Nick, who interceded only on matters requiring Courtney's active participation, pleading her delicate condition as an excuse. Her compliance reached its limit when Gina called, advocating a cake top that she had seen in the magazine. She had taken one look at the saucer-eyed juvenile bride and groom and let fly into Gina.

"Courtney, they're so cute!"

Cute. Nauseatingly so, Courtney fumed silently. "I

don't want to discuss it, Gina. Flowers only. No bride and groom of any sort. Got it?''

''But, Courtney . . .''

Courtney clenched her fists and took a deep breath, trying to restrain her temper. ''No, Gina. Absolutely not. And that's the end of it, you hear?''

Nick, seated beside her on the sofa, dropped his newspaper and pried the receiver from Courtney's white fingers just in time to hear his sister cry, ''But, Courtney, we're just trying to help you make a nice wedding!''

''I think we've had quite enough help. Enough is enough.''

''But, Nicky . . .''

''Gina, I want you to pass a message along to the others from me. If I have to deal with one more phone call like this, we'll elope the next day and there won't be a wedding.'' He paused to let his sister absorb the threat. ''Is that clear? Good. Good-bye.''

Before he could hang up the receiver, Gina's voice carried through the line. ''But what about the shower?''

He didn't answer her. If he had, he probably would have expanded his sister's vocabulary by three or four choice curse words.

FOURTEEN

"I'm going to kill them. Right there, in the middle of
St. Cecelia's, I'm going to pull an Uzi out from under my
wedding gown and blow them all away."

Selena stared, fascinated, as Courtney's eyes glimmered
erally. Julie, a seasoned veteran after twelve years of
witnessing such displays, just ignored her and picked at
her French fries.

"Can't you just picture it? Pink parasols and picture
ats and crinolines everywhere. It'll look like Sherman's
invasion of Georgia all over again. Except with Italians."

Julie chewed her bottom lip and tried not to laugh. It
wasn't easy—because she had seen the dresses.

"Court," she interjected reasonably, "don't you think
ou're overreacting, just a bit? After all, if you murder all
our in-laws, the baby's not going to have any relatives."

"I don't care. If the baby ever asks, we'll tell him they
ere all killed in a horrible accident."

"Just remember—I'm the one in the contrasting gown."

Selena eyed first one woman and then the other suspi-
ously. She didn't know either one of them well enough
be entirely sure they weren't serious about this. Cer-
inly, Nick's family had done everything humanly possi-

ble to warrant these women's speculation as to where they might acquire an Uzi.

"You know, Court," Julie remarked in an offhand manner, "I don't think you could fit an Uzi under your dress anymore."

Court looked at her balefully and sighed. Her size was a sensitive issue these days. "Couldn't leave well enough alone, could you? You had to mention it." She appealed to Selena. "You've been through this. Did you reach a point where you were certain you'd never see your feet again? And you wished you'd taken a closer look because you couldn't quite remember what they looked like?"

"I don't think I want to do this," Julie muttered under her breath.

Selena smiled and nodded, remembering. "Trust me, you will see your feet again and the varicose veins on the backs of your legs and the stretch marks and . . ."

Julie looked under the table, apparently for her purse.

"You're supposed to deliver in October, aren't you?" Selena asked Courtney.

"Orthopedic hose," Julie mumbled, considering her own sheer silk stockings.

"That's when my due date is, but nobody thinks I can make it that far," Courtney answered.

Julie looked under the table again.

"Steve's got a pool going. I've got a boy for the day after your wedding."

"Sensible shoes," Julie growled, inspecting one of her own Italian pumps.

"Bite your tongue." Courtney glared at Selena. "If this kid isn't born tomorrow, it's Nick's turn to carry it."

Julie looked under the table yet another time. This time Courtney and Selena both paused in their conversation to peer at her curiously.

Finally, Selena broke the silence. "Have you put the plastic under your sheets yet?"

Julie sat and stared silently at her plate.

"Not yet, but soon." Although she and Selena continued their conversation, both continued to watch Julie.

"We've been talking about another one. Talk's as far as we've gotten, though."

The color flowed from Julie's face and her eyes got very large.

"I don't think Nick dares to bring it up at this point. Even the priest didn't when we . . ." She paused to watch Julie swallow convulsively. ". . . went for counseling."

"Wise man," Selena remarked.

Grabbing her purse, Julie bolted from the table as Courtney and Selena stared after her.

After a few moments of silence, Selena asked, "Do you think one of us should go and see if she's all right?"

Courtney considered the question and shook her head. She began to giggle quietly.

Selena began, too, and when their eyes met, both women lost control.

After dropping Julie at her office, Courtney and Selena returned to Courtney's apartment, where they found Nick, Khalid, and Steve trying to assemble a high chair. From the looks of things, it was fortunate that they had months yet before the baby would be old enough to sit up in it.

"How much did you say they would have charged to put this thing together?" Steve demanded of Nick.

"Twenty-five dollars," Nick replied absently, concentrating on the sheet of directions.

"A bargain," Steve noted. "You should have taken ."

"Three college-educated adult men should be able to put together a high chair," Khalid insisted.

"Especially when one of them has done it once already," Selena observed.

"Maybe we should get Taylor here, too," Courtney added. "He'd probably be grateful for the practice."

Nick looked up from the directions and grinned. "Julie? The same Julie who went to buy bras with you?"

Courtney and Selena nodded.

"She had to leave lunch to get sick," Courtney informed the men gleefully, and she and Selena told the men all about it with the fiendish enthusiasm of two who had been through it themselves.

As the two women related the story of their lunch with Julie, first Khalid and then Nick joined in the laughter.

"You really are sick," Steve remarked, leaning back against the wall and looking around at the other four, who were all laughing.

"It's not sick," Khalid agreed. "You should have seen Selena the first time she made the morning dash. O.J Simpson couldn't have beaten her to the bathroom."

"Look who's laughing now," Selena retaliated. "I thought you were going to have heart failure at the time.'

"Sympathy, baby, sympathy," Khalid crooned, giving Nick a conspiratorial wink as he added, "You gotta tel them things like that to keep them happy."

Nick returned Khalid's smile half-heartedly, remember ing how he'd missed that part of Courtney's pregnancy He never should have waited all that time to come afte her. It had cost him so much that he could never replace watching the baby grow inside her, feeling its first move ments, even morning sickness . . . all the things tha bound couples together after they had children.

Courtney noted Nick's pensive frown and winced. Sh knew that Khalid and Selena had unwittingly hit a sor spot, reminding Nick of what he had missed. It was a her fault, she knew. After all, she had known that sh was pregnant when she had refused to see or talk to hin In spite of his repeated assertions that what had gor between them before his return was all in the past, sh didn't know how she could forgive her for everything sh had done.

"So, Courtney, do you like parties?" Steve's question interrupted their separate consideration of their regrets.

"Parties?" Courtney echoed, confused by the sudden change of subject.

"Parties. You know, liquor, dancing . . ."

Courtney looked down at her stomach meaningfully.

"All right, we'll give you a mineral water and you can pretend."

Nick's explanation clarified things for Courtney. "Kyle's coming a few days before the wedding with Trey, because Trey's got some convention at Columbia or something. I didn't catch exactly what it was all about."

"So we were thinking," Steve broke in eagerly, "that it'd be fun to get together then, without the monkey suits and all that wedding hoopla."

Courtney had to agree with Steve about the hoopla. Her hesitation must have lasted a beat too long, however, because Nick suggested hopefully, "We could have a nice cocktail buffet . . ."

Courtney's show of interest prompted him to add, "With hot and cold hors d'oeuvres . . ."

Courtney gave every appearance of considering his offer. He was so sweet, wanting to give her the party she had wanted before his family had gotten hold of their wedding.

". . . and steamed shrimp and miniature crab quiches . . ."

Although she tried to maintain the pretense of tough negotiator, her eyes misted over, ruining the illusion.

". . . and not a cookie in sight."

She smiled beatifically and sniffed. "I think we have a deal."

Nick tipped his dark head back, allowing the shower's spray to rinse the shampoo from his hair. He smiled gently as he recalled the look on Courtney's face when he'd described her fantasy wedding reception, the one his family had turned into "Royal Wedding, Part II." She'd looked so touched, so moved by the implied suggestion that they have another party just for them and their friends, without outside interference. He'd have to find out who Julie's caterer was.

As he lathered his chest for the shave that had been part of his daily ritual ever since he and Steve had begun wrestling, he mentally compiled a guest list, knowing he'd have to spend most of the next day on the telephone. Steve and Lord-only-knew what kind of date, Khalid and Selena, Julie and Taylor, Maggie, Kyle, Trey . . .

It came to him suddenly, unfortunately as he was just beginning with a razor, almost causing him to slice off his nipple. The wrestlers. Marty aka ''The Bulldozer'' and ''The Highland Warrior.'' Others, some of whom were even more outlandish. While Courtney appeared to have reconciled herself to the reality of his wrestling and there were some of the wrestlers, like Khalid and Steve, that she had even come to like, he wasn't sure if Courtney was ready for the rest of them as a group. If they were true to form in their behavior, they might give Courtney second thoughts about the wedding.

He searched the farthest recesses of his mind for a solution to the dilemma. The only one he could formulate was that he, Steve, and Khalid were going to have to see that the wrestlers were on their best behavior for the party. In short, there would have to be threats of permanent bodily harm made.

That much resolved, Nick returned the razor to his chest, making an additional mental note to hide the crystal

While Nick took his shower, Courtney stood in front of the open refrigerator, taking inventory of its contents and wishing that she had never permitted Nick to assume complete control of the food situation. While she didn't regret replacing take-out meals with his home cooking, his taste in snack foods left a great deal to be desired. For one thing, Nick did not share her belief that chocolate was on of the four basic food groups; instead, he kept buying her healthy things like fruit. As far as she was concerned, dried apricots were not an adequate substitute for a Milky Way. Nick's poor selection in snacks didn't detract from his excellent intuition, however; he had known that nothing he could give her would please her more than the reception she had wanted all along.

It was his ability to sense what she really wanted that she loved the most about him. Just as he had known about the party, he had known that she didn't really mean it when she told him to go away.

She had been an idiot, and only Nick's refusal to believe that what she said wasn't what she wanted had kept her from ruining both their lives. As it was, she had cheated them both of months they could have spent together, months in which they could have shared watching the baby grow, as Khalid and Selena had. She'd make it up to him if it was the last thing she did, even if it took the rest of both their lives. For starters, she could try getting along with his wrestling friends; after all, she liked the Abazas, didn't she?

That much determined, she shut the refrigerator door and opened the first kitchen cabinet, the one where she had always stashed her cookies pre-Nick. Sighing wearily, she stared at the void where they should have been, finally closed the door, and began searching for the Yellow Pages. She wondered, idly, if Haagen Dazs delivered.

The last few weeks before the wedding passed in a rush like a train without brakes.

Nick interceded in several minor skirmishes over flowers and the sudden snugness of Julie's gown; rented a car to drive Courtney, Julie, and Selena to the shower in Brooklyn and cheerfully made six pit stops en route; made all the cleaning and catering arrangements for the cocktail reception; and perpetually swore to Courtney that her only duty at the moment was to open presents and glow.

Courtney spent hours on the telephone reassuring Julie, who called every time she got sick; wrote thank-you notes to the Italian population of Brooklyn, the membership of the Fairfield Country Club, and Nick's wrestling federation; unpacked, with first apprehension and then delighted astonishment, the wrestlers' wedding present; and held her breath and waited for the train to crash.

Less than two hours before the guests were due to arrive for the cocktail reception, Courtney stood in front of the closet and considered her options. There weren't many. Most of the maternity clothes she'd purchased had been for work and, although she'd bought a few things for casual wear, she owned nothing that she considered festive enough for the occasion.

The week before, she and Julie had gone shopping, but she'd bought nothing. Not that she hadn't seen anything, but her innate practicality wouldn't allow her to pay real money for another outfit at this point in her pregnancy. Despite Julie's encouragement, which she suspected was motivated by a desire to borrow it somewhere down the road, she had resisted the urge to buy a gorgeous pants-and-top outfit that would have been perfect for the occasion.

Sighing, she reached for her safest choice, which she hadn't really liked when she had bought it. It didn't really matter these days because everything looked like a muumuu.

Behind her, Nick entered the bedroom. "Having a problem?"

"I don't have anything to wear," she muttered glumly, eyeing the dress in her hand and telling herself it wasn't really *that* bad of a choice.

"You sure about that?"

She turned and looked up suspiciously. He looked as if he knew something; more importantly, he was holding a large flat white dress box tied with a red satin bow.

"This was just delivered for you. I don't think it's a wedding present."

Courtney took the box from him, laid it on the bed, and lifted the lid slowly. Nested in a bed of tissue were the pants and top she and Julie had looked at the week before.

"Oh, Nick . . ." she wailed, beginning to tear up. "You shouldn't have . . ."

"Wasn't me, although I'd like to take credit for it . . . Read the card."

The message on the card read:

"Come on, I know you really like it. Stop being practical and live a little.

Julie

P.S. Can I borrow it sometime?"

Julie and Taylor were the first to arrive, and Julie raved enthusiastically about Courtney's outfit as if she'd never seen it before. Khalid and Selena followed shortly afterward, and then Steve, whose date was remarkable for the length of her legs and the brevity of her skirt. After them, wave after wave of people arrived, causing Courtney to wonder exactly how many people Nick had invited to this thing.

The number of wrestlers who had come to the party made Courtney nervous in spite of Nick's removal of all breakables that afternoon. She kept repeating to herself that people who had bought her and Nick service for twelve and completer pieces of Tiffany's "Monet" china pattern were unlikely to trash her apartment. As it turned out, the wrestlers got along amazingly well with her colleagues from work, contrary to her expectations that they would spend the evening standing on opposite sides of the room and glaring at each other like the Hatfields and McCoys.

All in all, the party seemed to be a success. Julie didn't throw up. Khalid showed Maggie pictures of his son and the new puppy. "The Bulldozer" demonstrated a head lock to one of Courtney's fellow associates. Steve and his date were nowhere to be seen, although Nick warned her, with the air of one who knows, not to open closets until they reappeared.

Courtney was chatting with Selena when the normal party din was shattered by the piercing whoop that was the Brawny Buccaneers' trademark. Courtney held her breath as she looked around cautiously, wondering which of Nick's wrestling friends was responsible and precisely how long it would be before the police responded to the neighbors' complaints. At last, she spotted the apparent culprits, the two men with whom Nick was exchanging elaborate handshakes that looked suspiciously fraternal in origin. One of the men, she recognized, was Kyle Phillips; the other, she assumed was Trey. It was a safe bet that Trey possessed the fourth tattoo.

With a broad smile, Nick towed them across the room to meet Courtney. She shook hands with Kyle, but before she could extend her hand to Trey, he placed his palm flat against her stomach in a way that seemed overly familiar for someone she just met.

When she looked down at his hand, he flushed, but he left it there. "Sorry. Occupational hazard."

"Excuse me?" she asked.

"He's an OB/GYN," Nick explained.

"Spontaneous?" Trey asked, looking up at Nick. He then answered his own question. "Of course it is. The wedding's Saturday."

"Spontaneous?" Nick echoed.

"Unassisted. Without help." As far as Courtney could tell, he didn't speak in whole sentences. "Just you and her in . . ."

"I understand," Nick interrupted, holding up one hand to stop him before he went further.

"Been a while since I've seen one. Specialize in infertility. When you due?'' He looked at Courtney's stomach, as if waiting for the baby to answer.

"October tenth," Courtney answered.

He considered it for a moment and shook his head. "Not a chance. Next week, tops."

"Sunday?" Selena asked hopefully.

"Maybe."

"Is it a boy?"

"Who was on top?"

In the aftermath of the party, Nick and Courtney cuddled on the sofa and surveyed the ruins. Although nothing was broken, the room showed the definite signs of hard use.

"Shut your eyes and don't think about it," Nick advised her. "I'll take care of it tomorrow."

She rubbed her cheek against his shoulder and murmured sleepily, "Okay."

"Do you have to be this agreeable now?"

She raised her head and smiled at him serenely.

He thought again how beautiful she was, with her violet eyes all smoky and sexy, her moist lips full and pink against her fair skin. He wanted her now even more than he had that first night back in the Poconos. Although he knew that was impossible, he bent his head to kiss her.

Their kiss was generous and demanding at the same time, with open mouths and tongues and teeth. He groaned as she nipped at his bottom lip and then soothed it with her tongue. She moaned as he sucked on her earlobe and moved down to the side of her throat. He shuddered when her hand pressed against his inner thigh. She trembled when his thumb caressed her nipple. Need grew in both of them until it raged like a bonfire.

When Courtney's hand moved again, it was more than Nick could bear. His hand closed around her wrist just as her fingers made contact with the hard ridge under his fly. With grim resolution, he raised her hand, pressed his open mouth to her palm, and placed it safely in her own lap. Rising from the sofa, he announced in a husky voice, "I'm going to go and take a shower."

As he stood under the cold spray minutes later, he hoped that Trey was right about his prediction that the baby would be born the following week and calculated exactly how long afterward he would have to continue taking cold showers.

Saturday morning dawned clear and beautiful, a picture book day for a wedding, Courtney told herself as she and Julie rode to Brooklyn in the limousine. Granted, there were a few deviations from the picture book conception of a wedding, such as the bride's huge stomach and aching back, and the maid of honor's irritated possession of a plastic bucket. Courtney fervently hoped they both made it through the wedding, although for the time being, she kept her doubts to herself.

As they passed each of the landmarks en route without incident, her confidence rose a notch; by the time they arrived at the church, she was convinced they could pull it off. Entering the bride's room at the church, however, brought back every one of her misgivings with a vengeance.

Chaos reigned, not that she'd expected anything else with the same bunch who'd been at her bridal fittings. Courtney's mother, Adele, looked positively frantic when she informed her that her father was outside chain-smoking, a habit he'd given up three years earlier. Courtney tried to tell her that the Trielos had that effect on people.

Julie bolted for the restroom, displacing the miniature bride, who promptly made a puddle on the new carpet. The flower girls, fearing that someone might have missed the event, made certain that everyone was aware of it. Gina and Lisa, meanwhile, liberated the electric rollers from the junior bridesmaids, engendering adolescent screams of outrage that they ignored. Anna Trielo, seated in the corner like the Queen Mother, beamed proudly as she observed the proceedings.

The ache in Courtney's back grew alarmingly sharper. In the chaos, only Adele noticed her swift intake of breath and sudden pallor. She peered at her daughter suspiciously and took her arm to steer her out into the hall. In all the confusion, they weren't missed.

It was blessedly quiet out there, and Courtney plopped into a nearby chair. Adele crouched down until she was at Courtney's eye level.

"You're in labor, aren't you?"

Courtney took a deep breath, tipped her head back against the wall, and closed her eyes.

"Courtney . . ." her mother demanded in the same voice she'd used when the Waterford bowl had mysteriously gotten chipped.

Courtney opened her eyes and raised her head to look at her mother as she admitted, "I think so."

"Think?"

"I'm pretty sure." She licked her lips and added, "My back hurts . . ."

She tried to describe it and Adele interrupted with a brisk nod. "That's labor."

Julie, wan and shaky, emerged from the bride's room. Courtney made an effort to get up to give her the chair because Julie looked as if she needed it more than she did. Frowning, Adele pushed her back and went and got another chair, which she placed beside Courtney's and Julie took gratefully.

Standing in front of them, Adele looked back and forth appraisingly. A glance at her watch told her that there was another half hour before the wedding. With the service itself and the ride back to Manhattan, she calculated a total of two hours, minimum, which was optimistic, since Courtney and Julie both still had to dress, put on make up, and do their hair. Neither of them looked capable of staying on her feet long enough to accomplish that. When

Courtney shifted uncomfortably in her chair again, Adele decided that there was only one course of action for her to take.

"I'll get Nick."

With that, she was gone, leaving the two women leaning against one another wearily like bookends.

"Lord, Court, I'm sorry," Julie groaned miserably. "I don't know how I'm going to . . ."

Courtney patted her arm reassuringly. "Don't worry, you won't have to."

"You're calling the wedding off again?" Julie's voice rose incredulously. "After . . ."

"I'm going to have the baby. Now."

Julie sat in stunned silence for a moment and then Courtney felt her shoulders shake with convulsive laughter.

"It's not funny," Courtney snapped.

Before Julie could insist that it was, Nick rounded the corner and hunkered down in front of Courtney, his hands on her stomach. He looked up at her and smiled wryly. "You know Gramma is never going to forgive you for this, don't you?"

Her violet eyes filled with tears and her bottom lip began to quiver threateningly.

"Sweetheart, don't . . ." He raised himself to kiss her lightly.

"But the wedding . . . all the money . . ."

He started to chuckle. Only a financial analyst would think of the expense at a time like this. "It doesn't matter, honey."

Steve and Trey rushed up and Trey knelt down beside her, elbowing Nick out of the way. After a cursory examination and a few questions, he turned to Nick. "Your doctor back in the city?"

Nick nodded.

"Call the doctor. Let's get going."

"I'll call," Steve offered, "if you give me the number."

As Nick fished the doctor's card out of his wallet and handed it to Steve, Trey looked at Julie. "You look lousy. Try soda crackers."

Nick scooped Courtney into his arms and turned just as Gina stuck her head through the door of the bride's room. Someone, probably his grandmother, had finally noticed the absence of the bride, her mother, and the maid of honor. Gina shrieked when she saw him. "You aren't supposed to be here! You aren't supposed to see her before the wedding!"

Nick ignored her as he hurried away with Courtney.

"You can't leave now! The wedding's in half an hour!"

Trey calmly dug a package of crackers out of his pocket and offered them to Julie. "Think we should go along?"

She nodded and stood. With the plastic bucket in one hand, she took his arm and the two of them followed after Nick and Courtney.

"But what do we tell everyone?" Gina demanded frantically.

Trey turned and looked back at Nick's sister. "That if we leave now, we might make it to the hospital before Courtney delivers."

As planned, the following day's newspapers published the announcement of the marriage of Miss Courtney Ann Welsch and Mr. Nicholas Anthony Trielo. Because the article had been written days earlier, however, as society pages are, the wedding described in the announcement bore little resemblance to the wedding that actually took place.

Nick and Courtney were not united in matrimony in a double ring service before seven hundred in St. Cecelia's Roman Catholic Church in Brooklyn. The bride, who was not clad in satin and Bordeaux lace, was not given in marriage by her father. She was not attended by a fleet of bridesmaids, junior bridesmaids, and flower girls in floral dresses. There was no miniature bride. The groomsmen did not wear ensembles that coordinated with the women's clothing. There was no music, nor were there flowers.

Instead, assured by Trey that they had plenty of time, Father Castagna performed the ceremony in the back seat of the limousine on the way to the hospital in Manhattan. There were only six people present, Father Castagna, Adele, Trey, Julie, Nick, and Courtney, but it was extremely crowded nonetheless. Courtney, who was still wearing her blue shorts, Nick's T-shirt, and Reeboks, was given away by Adele and attended by Julie, also in shorts and still carrying her plastic bucket. Trey, who acted as best man, had more to do in his other role as physician. The rings, like Courtney's father, had been forgotten back at the church.

Because the bride and groom were otherwise occupied and unable to attend, the reception was held without them. With all the chicken and ziti and cookies ready, and the guests all there, Gramma Trielo thought that it was the least they could do to feed them and the rest of the family, who had anticipated a party for weeks, agreed enthusiastically.

Kyle and Feroher played and everyone ate and drank and danced. After a few drinks, Taylor and Courtney's father took a cab to the hospital to join their wives. Selena and Khalid decided they really should have a second baby and went home early to work on it. Steve and "The Bulldozer" left with two of the secretaries from Courtney's office. Nick's fellow wrestlers deposited Jason Becker in a convenient fountain while Maggie cheered them on. Everyone had such a good time that Gramma Trielo pronounced the wedding a roaring success.

In the years to come, when she told her friends about her grandson Nicky's wedding, Gramma Trielo would forget to mention that Nicky and his bride hadn't been at either the wedding or the reception. If anyone were so bold as to challenge her memory about the event, she would haul out the huge white and gold wedding album that she had put together for Nick and Courtney, just as she had for her other grandchildren when they got married. Inside were the neatly clipped and mounted newspaper announcements, which documented the wedding precisely as she remembered it. And if anyone questioned the lack of photographs, she showed them the sprig of flowers from Courtney's bouquet and the piece of Bordeaux lace from Courtney's gown. And if they continued to pursue the issue, she proudly showed them the last page in the book, which bore the birth announcement, first photograph, and footprint of Nicholas Anthony Trielo, Jr., the first Trielo great-grandchild. She always did so with a gleam in her eye that dared the listener to point out that the baby had been born at 12:06 the morning after the wedding.

No one dared.

EPILOGUE

"Nick?"

Although he was half asleep, sated with both turkey and Courtney, he came alert instantly. They knew, he thought. Somehow his family had found out that they hadn't gone to the Welsches for Thanksgiving but were, instead, spending it alone with their son. "Yes, Court?" he asked fearfully.

"I was thinking the other day about going back to work . . ."

He stopped holding his breath, telling himself that paranoia wasn't an attractive trait. "And?"

"I don't really want to go."

He'd suspected as much, although he hadn't wanted to be the first one to mention it; she had rejected twenty-six perfectly qualified applicants for the position of nanny. "Court, you don't have to go back to work if you don' want to. It's not like we need the money."

She sat up in bed and pulled on an oversize "Brawn" Buccaneers" T-shirt that she sometimes wore to keep he back warm. It served its function so well that it also kep him warm when she wore it.

He sat up, too, his back against the headboard, and towed her between his legs, her back against his chest.

"It's not the money . . ."

"You want the partnership." He massaged her back as she thought, so absorbed that she didn't notice when he slipped the back of the shirt up to expose her to her shoulder blades.

"Yes, but I keep thinking that it might not be worth it. I'm having a better time with Nicky than I expected . . ."

"So then, extend the leave of absence." He took advantage of her distraction to slide his hands around her sides to the undersides of her breasts.

"Actually, I was thinking about starting my own office," Courtney said bluntly and quickly.

Nick's hands halted mid-grope. He really didn't know what to say at the moment, the idea was so out of the blue.

"I saw this brownstone the other day on the East Side while I was out walking Nicky . . ." she began hesitantly. "It has an office already because a doctor had it before . . ." Her words gained momentum as she continued and Nick maintained his silence, allowing her to speak. ". . . and because he lived there, it's all attached. I wouldn't have to leave Nicky because I could just work from there. And I know that Maggie would come to work for me if I asked her. I don't know exactly how many of my clients would come with me . . ."

"How much do they want for it?" he asked, knowing full well that the idea had gone well beyond mere speculation.

She named a price that took his breath.

"It *is* on the East Side," she defended, twisting in his arms so that she could watch his reactions. He still looked uncomfortable with the amount. "And the payments would only be a hundred dollars more a month than we pay for this apartment. Half of which would be tax-deductible."

The idea started to sound reasonable, and the expression on his face reflected it.

"If we put in an office for the 'Brawny Buccaneers,' two-thirds."

"Really?"

"Really."

"How many bedrooms?"

"Five. All hardwood floors. Several stained glass windows. Original wall sconces." Her eyes gleamed.

Nick smiled at her, aware that the idea had gone as far as calling the realtor and seeing the brownstone. "Room for a dog?"

She returned his smile radiantly and nodded.

"Can we look at it tomorrow?"

She nodded again. "Eleven o'clock."

Laughing, Nick slid his hands up her body, slipped the T-shirt over her head, and began nuzzling on the nape of her neck. Courtney turned in his arms and pushed him back, pinning his shoulders against the pillow. As she lowered her mouth to his, he asked, "Are we working on filling the other three bedrooms?"

SHARE THE FUN . . .
SHARE YOUR NEW-FOUND TREASURE!!

You don't want to let your new books out of your sight? That's okay. Your friends can get their own. Order below.

No. 5 A LITTLE INCONVENIENCE by Judy Christenberry
Never one to give up easily, Liz overcomes every obstacle Jason throws in her path and loses her heart in the process.

No. 6 CHANGE OF PACE by Sharon Brondos
Police Chief Sam Cassidy was everyone's protector but could he protect himself from the green-eyed temptress?

No. 7 SILENT ENCHANTMENT by Lacey Dancer
She was elusive and she was beautiful. Was she real? She was Alex's true-to-life fairy-tale princess.

No. 8 STORM WARNING by Kathryn Brocato
The tempest on the outside was mild compared to the raging passion of Valerie and Devon—and there was no warning!

No. 13 SIEGE OF THE HEART by Sheryl McDanel Munson
Nick pursues Court while she wrestles with her heart and mind.

No. 14 TWO FOR ONE by Phyllis Herrmann
What is it about Cal and Elliot that has Leslie seeing double?

No. 15 A MATTER OF TIME by Anne Bullard
Does Josh *really* want Christine or is there something else?

No. 16 FACE TO FACE by Shirley Faye
Christi's definitely not Damon's type. So, what's the attraction?
